HERE AND NOW STORY BOOK

TWO- TO SEVEN-YEAR-OLDS

Experimental Stories Written for the Children of
the City and Country School (formerly the Play
School) and the Nursery School of the Bureau of
Educational Experiments.

BY

LUCY SPRAGUE MITCHELL

ILLUSTRATED BY

HENDRIK WILLEM VAN LOON

CONTENTS

FOREWORD

Our school has always assumed that children are interested in and will work with or give expression to those things which are familiar to them. This is not new: the kindergarten gives domestic life a prominent place with little children. But with the kindergarten the present and familiar is abandoned in most schools and emphasis is placed upon that which is unfamiliar and remote. It is impossible to conceive of children working their own way from the familiar to the unknown unless they develop a method in understanding the familiar which will apply to the unfamiliar as well. This method is the method of art and science—the method of experimentation and inquiry. We can almost say that children are born with it, so soon do they begin to show signs of applying it. As they have been in the past and as they are in the present to a very great extent, schools make no attempt to provide for this method; in fact they take pains to introduce another. They are disposed to set up a rigid program which answers inquiries before they are made and supplies needs before they have been felt.

We try to keep the children upon present day and familiar things until they show by their attack on materials and especially upon information that they are ready to work out into the unknown and unfamiliar. In the matter of stories and verse which fit into such a program we have always felt an almost total void. Whether other schools feel this would depend upon their intentional program. Surely no school would advise giving classical literature without the setting which would make the stories and verse understandable. It is a question whether the fact of desirable literature has not in the past and does not still govern our whole school program more than many educators would be willing to admit. What seems to be more logical is to set up that which is psychologically sound so far as we know it and create if need be a new literature to help support the structure.

In the presence of art, schools have always taken a modest attitude. For some reason or other they seem to think it out of their province. They regard children as potential scientists, professional men and women, captains of industry, but scarcely potential artists. To what school of design, what academy of music, what school of literary production, do our common schools lead? We are not fitting our children to compose, to create, but at our best to appreciate and reproduce.

Mrs. Mitchell as story teller in this new sense of writing stories, rather than merely telling them, is having an influence in the school which has not been altogether unlooked for. The children look upon themselves as composers in language and language thus becomes not merely a useful medium of expression but also an art medium. They regard their own content, gathered by themselves in a perfectly familiar setting as fit for use as art material. That is, just as the children draw and show power to compose with crayons and paints, they use language to compose what they term stories or occasionally, verse. Often these "stories" are a mere rehearsal of experiences, but in so far as they are vivid and have some sort of fitting ending they pass as a childish art expression just as their compositions in drawing do.

So far as content is concerned the school gives the children varied opportunities to know and express what they find in their environment. Mrs. Mitchell finds this content in the school. It is being used, it is even being expressed in language. What she particularly does is to show the possibility of using this same content as art in language. She does this both by writing stories herself and by helping the children to write. The children are not by any means read to, so much as they are encouraged to tell their own stories. These are taken down verbatim by the teachers of the younger groups. Through skilful handling of several of the older groups what the children call "group stories" are produced as well as individual ones.

We hope this book will bring to parents and teachers what it has to us, a new method of approach to literature for little children, and to children the joy our children have in the stories themselves.

CAROLINE PRATT

The City and Country School
July, 1921

HERE AND NOW STORY BOOK

HERE AND NOW STORY BOOK

INTRODUCTION

These stories are experiments,—experiments both in content and in form. They were written because of a deep dissatisfaction felt by a group of people working experimentally in a laboratory school, with the available literature for children. I am publishing them not because I feel they have come through to any particularly noteworthy achievement, but because they indicate a method of work which I believe to be sound where children are concerned. They must always be regarded as experiments, but experiments which have been strictly limited to lines suggested to me by the children themselves. Both the stuff of the stories and the mould in which they are cast are based on suggestions gained directly from children. I have tried to put aside my notions of what was "childlike." I have tried to ignore what I, as an adult, like. I have tried to study children's

1

interests not historically but through their present
observations and inquiries, and their sense of form
through their spontaneous expressions in language,
and to model my own work strictly on these find-
ings. I have forced myself throughout to be de-
liberate, conscious, for fear I should slip back to
adult habits of thought and expression. I can give
here only samples of the many stories and questions I have gathered from the children which
form the basis of my own stories. Suffice it that
my own stories attempt to follow honestly the leads
which here and now the children themselves indicate in content and in form, no matter how difficult
or strange the going for adult feet.

First, as to the stuff of which the story is made,—
the content. I have assumed that anything to
which a child gives his spontaneous attention, anything which he questions as he moves around the
world, holds appropriate material about which to
talk to him either in speech or in writing. I have
assumed that the answers to these his spontaneous
inquiries should be given always in terms of a
relationship which is natural and intelligible at
his age and which will help him to order the
familiar facts of his own experiences. Thus the
answers will themselves lead him on to new inquiries. For they will give him not so much new

facts as a new method of attack. I have further
assumed that any of this material which by taking
on a pattern form can thereby enhance or deepen
its intrinsic quality is susceptible of becoming
literature. Material which does not lend itself to
some sort of intentional design or form, may be
good for informational purposes but not for stories
as such.

The task, then, is to examine first the things
which get the spontaneous attention of a two-year-
old, a three-year-old and so up to a seven-year-
old; and then to determine what relationships are
natural and intelligible at these ages. Obviously
to determine the mere subject of attention is not
enough. Children of all ages attend to engines.
But the two-year-old attends to certain things and
the seven-year-old to quite different ones. The
relationships through which the two-year-old interprets his observations may make of the engine
a gigantic extension of his own energy and move-
..ent; whereas the relationships through which the
seven-year-old interprets his observations may
make of the engine a scientific example of the ex-
pansion of steam or of the desire of men to get
rapidly from one place to another. What relationship he is relying on we can get only by watching the child's own activities. The second part

of the task is to discover what *is* pattern to the
untrained but unspoiled ears, eyes, muscles and
minds of the little folk who are to consume the
stories. Each part of the task has its peculiar diffi-
culties. But fortunately in each, children do point
the way if we have the courage to forget our own
adult way and follow theirs.

CONTENT

In looking for content for these stories I followed the general lines of the school for which
they were written. The school gives the children
the opportunity to explore first their own environment and gradually widens this environment for
them along lines of their own inquiries. Consequently I did not seek for material outside the ordinary surroundings of the children. On the
contrary, I assumed that in stories as in other educational procedure, the place to begin is the point
at which the child has arrived,—to begin and lead
out from. With small children this point is still
within the "here" and the "now," and so stories
must begin with the familiar and the immediate.
But also stories must lead children out from the
familiar and immediate, for that is the method
both of education and of art. Here and now sto-

ries mean to me stories which include the children's first-hand experiences as a starting point, not stories which are literally limited to these experiences. Therefore to get my basis for the stories I went to the environment in which a child of each age naturally finds himself and there I watched him. I tried to see what in his home, in his school, in the streets, he seized upon and how he made this his own. I tried to determine what were the relationships he used to order his experiences. Fortunately for the purposes of writing stories I did not have to get behind the baffling eyes and the inscrutable sounds of a small baby. Yet I learned much for understanding the twos by watching even through the first months. What "the great, big, blooming, buzzing confusion" (as James describes it) means to an infant, I fancy we grown-ups will really never know. But I suppose we may be sure that existence is to him largely a stream of sense impressions. Also I suppose we are reasonably safe in saying that whatever the impression that reaches him he tends to translate it into action. At what age a child accomplishes what can be called a "thought" or what these first thoughts are, is surely beyond our present powers to describe. But that his early thoughts have a discernible muscular expression, I fancy we may

say. It may well be that thought is merely asso-
ciative memory as Loeb maintains. It may well
be that behaviorists are right and that thought is
just "the rhythmic mimetic rehearsal of the first
hand experience in motor terms." If the act of
thinking is itself motor, its expression is somewhat
attenuated in adults. Be that as it may, a small
child's expressions are still in unmistakable motor
terms. It is obviously through the large muscles
that a baby makes his responses. And even a three-
year-old can scarcely think "engine" without showing the pull of his muscles and the puff-puffing of
exertion. Nor can he observe an object without
making some movement towards it. He takes in
through his senses; and he interprets through his
muscles.

For our present purposes this characteristic has
an important bearing. The world pictured for the
child must be a world of sounds and smells and
tastes and sights and feeling and contacts. Above
all his early stories must be of activities and they
must be told in motor terms. Often we are tempted
to give him reasons in response to his incessant
"why?" but when he asks "why?" he really is
not searching for reasons at all. A large part of
the time he is not even asking a question. He
merely enjoys this reciperative form of speech and

is indignant if your answer is not what he expects. One of my children enjoyed this antiphonal method of following his own thoughts to such an extent that for a time he told his stories in the form of questions telling me each time what to answer! His questions had a social but no scientific bearing. And even when a three-year-old asks a real question he wants to be answered in terms of action or of sense impressions and not in terms of reasons why. How could it be otherwise since he still thinks with his senses and his muscles and not with that generalizing mechanism which conceives of cause and effect? The next time a three-year-old asks you "why you put on shoes?" see if he likes to be told "Mother wears shoes when she goes out because it is cold and the sidewalks are hard," or if he prefers, "Mother's going to go outdoors and take a big bus to go and buy something:" or "You listen and in a minute you'll hear mother's shoes going pat, pat, pat downstairs and then you'll hear the front door close bang! and mother won't be here any more!" "Why?" really means, "please talk to me!" and naturally he likes to be talked to in terms he can understand which are essentially sensory and motor.

Now what activities are appropriate for the first stories? I think the answer is clear. His, the child's, own! The first activities which a child knows are of course those of his own body movements whether spontaneous or imposed upon him by another. Everything is in terms of himself. Again I think none of us would like to hazard a guess as to when the child comes through to a sharp distinction between himself and other things or other persons. But we are sure, I think, that this distinction is a matter of growth which extends over many years and that at two, three, and even four, it is imperfectly apprehended. We all know how long a child is in acquiring a correct use of the pronouns "me" and "you." And we know that long after he has this language distinction, he still calls everything he likes "mine." "This is my cow, this is my tree!" The only way to persuade him that it is *not* his is to call it some one else's. Possessed it must be. He knows the world only in personal terms. That is, his early sense of relationship is that of himself to his concrete environment. This later evolves into a sense of relationship between other people and their concrete environment.

At first, then, a child can not transcend himself or his experiences. Nor should he be asked to. A two-year-old's stories must be completely his

stories with his own familiar little person moving
in his own familiar background. They should
vivify and deepen the sense of the one relationship
he does feel keenly,—that of himself to something
well-known. Now a two-year-old's range of experiences is not large. At least the experiences in
which he takes a real part are not many. So his
stories must be of his daily routine,—his eating,
his dressing, his activities with his toys and his
home. These are the things to which he attends:
they make up his world. And they must be his
very own eating and dressing and home, and not
eating and dressing and homes in general. Stories
which are not intimately his own, I believe either
pass by or strain a two-year-old; and I doubt
whether many three-year-olds can participate with
pleasure and without strain in any experience
which has not been lived through in person. He
may of course get pleasure from the sound of the
story apart from its meaning much earlier. Just
now we are thinking solely of the content. I well
remember the struggles of my three-year-old boy
to get outside himself and view a baby chicken's
career objectively. He checked up each step in
my story by this orienting remark, "That the baby
chicken in the shell, not me! The baby chicken

go scritch-scratch, not me!" Was not this an
evident effort to comprehend an extra-personal
relationship?

Again just as at first a small child can not get
outside himself, so he can not get outside the immediate. At first he can not by himself recall even
a simple chronological sequence. He is still in
the narrowest, most limiting sense, too entangled
in the "here" and the "now." The plot sense
emerges slowly. Indeed there is slight plot value
in most children's stories up to eight years. Plot
is present in embryonic form in the omnipresent
personal drama: "Where's baby? Peek-a-boo!
There she is!" It can be faintly detected in the
pleasure a child has in an actual walk. But the
pleasure he derives from the sense of complete-
ness, the sense that a walk or a story has a beginning and a middle and an end, the real plot
pleasure, is negligible compared with the pleasure
he gets in the action itself. Small children's experiences are and should be pretty much continuous flows of more or less equally important
episodes. Their stories should follow their experiences. They should have no climaxes, no sense of
completion. The episodes should be put together
more like a string of beads than like an organic
whole. Almost any section of a child's experience

related in simple chronological sequence makes a satisfactory story.

This can be pressed even further. There is another kind of relationship by which little children interpret their environment. It is the early manifestation of the associational process which in our adult life so largely crowds out the sensory and motor appreciation of the world. It runs way back to the baby's pleasure in recognizing things, certainly long before the period of articulate questions. We all retain vestiges of this childlike pleasure in our joyful greeting of a foreign word that is understood or in any new application of an old thought or design. As a child acquires a few words he adds the pleasure of naming,—an extension of the pleasure of recognition. This again develops into the joy of enumerating objects which are grouped together in some close association, usually physical juxtaposition. For instance a two- or three-year-old likes to have every article he ate for breakfast rehearsed or to have every member of the family named at each episode in a story which concerns the group! Earlier he likes to have his five little toes checked off as pigs or merely numbered. This is closely tied up with the child's pattern sense which we shall discuss at length under "Form." Now the pleasure of

enumeration, like that of a refrain, is in part at
least a pleasure in muscle pattern. My two-year-
old daughter composed a song which well illus-
trates the fascination of enumeration. The refrain
"Tick-tock" was borrowed from a song which had
been sung to her.

> "Tick-tock
>   Marni's nose,
> Tick-tock
>   Marni's eyes,
> Tick-tock
>   Marni's mouth,
> Tick-tock
>   Marni's teeth,
> Tick-tock
>   Marni's chin,
> Tick-tock
>   Marni's romper,
> Tick-tock
>   Marni's stockings,
> Tick-tock
>   Marni's shoes," etc., etc.

This she sang day after day, enumerating such
groups as her clothes, the objects on the mantel and
her toys. Walt Whitman has given us glorified

enumerations of the most astounding vitality. If some one would only pile up equally vigorous ones for children! But it is not easy for an adult to gather mere sense or motor associations without a plot thread to string them on. The children's response to the two I have attempted in this collection, "Old Dan" and "My Kitty," make me eager to see it tried more commonly.

All this means that the small child's attention and energy are absorbed in developing a technique of observation and control of his immediate surroundings. The functioning of his senses and his muscles engrosses him. Ideally his stories should happen currently along with the experience they relate or the object they reproduce, merely deepening the experience by giving it some pleasurable expression. At first the stories will have to be of this running and partly spontaneous type. But soon a child will like to have the story to recall an experience recently enjoyed. The living over of a walk, a ride, the sight of a horse or a cow, will give him a renewed sense of participation in a pleasurable activity. This is his first venture in vicarious experiences. And he must be helped to it through strong sense and muscular recalls. I have felt that these fairly literal recalls of every day details *did* deepen his sense of relationships since by himself he cannot recapture these familiar details even in a simple chronological sequence.

But if stories for a two or a three-year-old need to be of himself they must be written especially for him. Those written for another two-year-old may not fit. Consequently the first three stories in this collection are given as types rather than as independent narratives. "Marni Takes a Ride" is so elementary in its substance and its form as to be hardly recognizable as a "story" at all. And yet the appeal is the same as in the more developed narratives. It falls between the embryonic story stage of "Peek-a-boo!" and Marni's second story. It was first told during the actual ride. Repeated later it seemed to give the child a sense of adventure,—an inclusion of and still an extension of herself beyond the "here" and "now" which is the essence of a story. Both of Marni's stories are given as types for a mother to write for her two-year-old; the "Room with the Window in It" (written for the Play School group) is given as a type for a teacher to write for her three-year-old group.

I cannot leave the subject of the "familiar" for children without looking forward a few years. This process of investigating and trying to control his immediate surroundings, this appreciation of the world through his senses and his muscles, does not end when the child has gained some sense of his own self as distinguished from the world,—of the "me" and the "not me,"—or achieved some ability to expand temporarily the "here" and the "now" into the "there" and the "then." The process is a precious one and should not be interrupted and confused by the interjection of remote or impersonal material. He still thinks and feels primarily through his own immediate experiences. If this is interfered with he is left without his natural material for experimentation for he cannot yet experiment easily in the world of the intangible. Moreover to the child the familiar *is* the interesting. And it remains so I believe through that transition period,—somewhere about seven years, —when the child becomes poignantly aware of the world outside his own immediate experience,—of an order, physical or social, which he does not determine, and so gradually develops a sense of standards of what is to be expected in the world of nature or of his fellows along with a sense of workmanship. It is only the blind eye of the adult that finds the familiar uninteresting. The attempt to amuse children by presenting them with the strange, the bizarre, the unreal, is the unhappy

result of this adult blindness. Children do not
find the unusual piquant until they are firmly
acquainted with the usual; they do not find the
preposterous humorous until they have intimate
knowledge of ordinary behavior; they do not get
the point of alien environments until they are se-
curely oriented in their own. Too often we
mistake excitement for genuine interest and give
the children stimulus instead of food. The fairy
story, the circus, novelty hunting, delight the
sophisticated adult; they excite and confuse the
child. Red Riding-Hood and circus Indians excite the little child; Cinderella confuses him. Not
one clarifies any relationship which will further
his efforts to order the world. Nonsense when
recognized and enjoyed as such is more than legitimate; it is a part of every one's heritage. But nonsense which is confused with reality is vicious,—
the more so because its insinuations are subtle.
So far as their content is concerned, it is chiefly
as a protest against this confusing presentation of
unreality, this substitution of excitement for legitimate interest, that these stories have been written.
It is not that a child outgrows the familiar. It is
rather that as he matures, he sees new relationships
in the old. If our stories would follow his lead,
they should not seek for unfamiliar and strange

stuff in intrigue him; they should seek to deepen
and enrich the relationships by which he is dimly
groping to comprehend and to order his familiar
world.

But to return to the younger children. Children
of four are not nearly so completely ego-centric as
those of three. There has seemed to me to be a
distinct transition at this age to a more objective
way of thinking. A four-year-old does not to the
same extent have to be a part of every situation he
conceives of. Ordinarily, too, he moves out from
his own narrowly personal environment into a
slightly wider range of experiences. Now, what
in this wider environment gets his spontaneous attention? What does he take from the street life,
for instance, to make his own? Surely it is moving
things. He is still primarily motor in his interest
and expression and remains so certainly up to six
years. Engines, boats, wagons with horses, all animals, his own moving self,—these are the things
he notices and these are the things he interprets
in his play activities. Transportation and animals
and himself. Do not these pretty well cover the
field of his interests? If conceived of as motor
and personal do they not hold all the material a
four- or five-year-old needs for stories? If we bring
in inanimate unmoving things, we must do with

them what he does. We must endow them with life and motion. We need not be afraid of personification. This is the age when anthropomorphism flourishes. The five-year-old is still motor; his conception of cause is still personal. He thinks through his muscles; he personifies in his thought and his play.

Nevertheless there is very real danger in anthropomorphism,—in thus leaving the world of reality. There is danger of confusing the child. We must be sure our personifications are built on relationships which our child can understand and which have an objective validity. We must be sure that a wolf remains a wolf and an engine an engine, though endowed with human speech.

Now, what are the typical relationships which a four- or five-year-old uses to bind together his world into intelligible experiences? We have already noted the personal relationship which persists in modified form. But does not the grouping of things because of physical juxtaposition now give way to a conception of "Use"? Does he not think of the world largely in terms of active functioning? Has not the typical question of this age become "What's it for?" Even his early definitions are in terms of use which has a strong motor implication. "A table is to eat off"; "a spoon is to

eat in"; "a river means where you get drinks out
of water, and catch fish, and throw stones." (Wad-
dle: Introduction to Child Psychology, p. 170.)
It was only consistent with his general conception
of relationships in the world to have a little boy
of my acquaintance examine a very small man sitting beside him in the subway and then turn to
his father with the question, "What is that little
man for?"

Stories which are offered to small children must
be assessed from this two-fold point of view. What
relationships are they based on? And in what
terms are they told? Fairy stories should not be
exempted. We are inclined to accept them un-
critically, feeling that they do not cramp a child
as does reality. We cling to the idea that children
need a fairy world to "cultivate their imagina-
tions." In the folk tales we are intrigued by the
past,—by the sense that these embodiments of
human experience, having survived the ages,
should be exempt from modern analysis. If, however, we do commit the sacrilege of looking at them
alongside of our educational principles, I think we
find a few precious ones that stand the test. For
children under six, however, even these precious
few contribute little in content, but much through
their matchless form. On the other hand, we find

that many of the human experiences which these old tales embody are quite unsuitable for four- and five-year-olds. Cruelty, trickery, economic inequality,—these are experiences which have shaped and shaken adults and alas! still continue to do so. But do we wish to build them into a four-year-old's thinking? Some of these experiences run counter to the trends of thinking we are trying to establish in other ways; some merely confuse them. We seem to identify imagination with gullibility or vague thinking. But surely true imagination is not based on confusion. Imagination is the basis of art. But confused art is a contradiction of terms.

Now, the ordinary fairy tale which is the chief story diet of the four- and five-year-olds, I believe does confuse them; not because it does not stick to reality (for neither do the children) but because it does not deal with the things with which they have had first-hand experience and does not attempt to present or interpret the world according to the relationships which the child himself employs. Rather it gives the child material which he is incapable of handling. Much in these tales is symbolic and means to the adult something quite different from what it bears on its face. And much, I believe, is confused even to the grown-up.

Now a confused adult does not make a child! Nor
does it ever help a child to give him confusion.
When my four-year-old personified a horse for one
whole summer, he lived the actual life of a horse
as far as he knew it. His bed was always "a stall,"
his food was always "hay," he always brushed his
"mane" and "put on his harness" for breakfast. It
was only when real horse information gave out
that he supplied experiences from his own life.
He was not limited by reality. He was exercising
his imagination. This is quite different from the
adult mixtures of the animal, the social, and the
moral worlds. Does not Cinderella interject a
social and economic situation which is both confusing and vicious? Does not Red Riding-Hood
in its real ending plunge the child into an inappropriate relationship of death and brutality or in
its "happy ending" violate all the laws that can be
violated in regard to animal life? Does not "Jack
and the Beanstalk" delay a child's rationalizing of
the world and leave him longer than is desirable
without the beginnings of scientific standards?
The growth of the sense of reality is a growth of
the sense of relations. From the time when the
child begins to relate isolated experiences, when
he groups together associations, when he begins to
note the sequence, the order of things, from this

time he is beginning to think scientifically. It is preëminently the function of education to further the growth of the sense of reality, to give the child the sense of relationship between facts, material or social: that is, to further scientific conceptions. Stories, if they are to be a part of an educational process, must also further the growth of the sense of reality, must help the child to interpret the relationships in the world around him and help him to develop a scientific process of thinking. It is not important that he know this or that particular fact; it *is* important that he be able to fit any particular fact into a rational scheme of thought. Accordingly, the relationships which a story clarifies are of much greater import than the facts it gives. All this, of course, concerns the content of stories— the intentional material it presents to the child and has nothing to do with the pleasure of the presentation,—the relish which comes from the form of the story. I do not wish this to be interpreted to mean that I think all fairy stories forever harmful. From the beginning innocuous tales like the "Gingerbread Man" should be given for the pattern as should the "Old Woman and Her Pig." Moreover, after a child is somewhat oriented in the physical and social world, say at six or seven,— I think he can stand a good deal of straight fairy

lore. It will sweep him with it. He will relish
the flight the more for having had his feet on the
ground. But for brutal tales like Red Riding-
Hood or for sentimental ones like Cinderella I find
no place in any child's world. Obviously, fairy
stories cannot be lumped and rejected en masse.
I am merely pleading not to have them accepted en
masse on the ground that they "have survived the
ages" and "cultivate the imagination." For a
child's imagination, since it is his native endow-
ment, will surely flourish if he is given freedom
for expression, without calling upon the stimulus
of adult fancies. It is only the jaded adult mind,
afraid to trust to the children's own fresh springs
of imagination, that feels for children the need of
the stimulus of magic.

The whole question of myths and sagas together
with the function of personification must be taken
up with the older children. For the present we
are still concerned with four- and five-year-olds.
Two sets of stories told by four- and five-year-old
children in the school seem to me to show what
emphasizing unrealities may do at this age. The
first child in each set is thinking disjunctively;
the second has his facts organized into definite relationships. Can one think that the second child
enjoyed his ordered world less than the first enjoyed his confusion?

Two Stories by Four-Year-Olds

Once there was a table and he was taking a walk and he fell into a pond of water and an alligator bit him and then he came up out of the pond of water and he stepped into a trap that some hunters had set for him, and turned a somersault on his nose.

There was a new engine and it didn't have any headlight—its light wasn't open in its headlight so its engineer went and put some fire in the wires and made a light. And then it saw a lot of other engines on the track in front of it. So when it wanted to puff smoke and go fast it told its engineer and he put some coal in the coal car. And then the other engines told their engineers to put coal in their coal cars and then they all could go.

(The child then played a song by a " 'lectric" engine on the piano and tried to write the notes.)

Two Stories by Five-Year-Olds

Once upon a time there was a clown and the clown jumped on the bed and the bed jumped on the cup. Then the clown took a pencil and drawed on his face. And the clown said, "Oh, I guess I'll sit in a rocking chair." So the rocking chair said, "Ha! ha!" and it tumbled away. Then a little pig came along and he said, "Could you throw me up and throw an apple down?" So the clown threw him so far that he was dead. He was on the track.

There was a big factory where all the men made engines. And one man made a smoke stack. And one man made a tender. And one man made a cab. And one man made a bell. And one man made a wheel. And then another man came and put them all together and made a great big engine. And this man said, "We haven't any tracks!" And then a man came and made the tracks. And then another man said, "We haven't any station!" So many men came and built a big station. And they said, "Let's have the station in Washington Square." So they pulled down the Arch and they pulled up all the sidewalks. And they built a big station. And they left all the houses; for where would we live else?

(In a sequel he says: So they knocked down the Arch and chopped up all the pieces. And they chopped all around the trees but they didn't chop them down because they looked so pretty with our station!)

I am far from meaning that five-year-olds should be confined to their literal experiences. They have made considerable progress in separating themselves from their environment though at times they seem still to think of the things around them more or less as extensions of themselves. Their inquiries still emanate from their own personal experiences; but they do not end there. A child of this age has a genuine curiosity about where things come from and where they go to. "What's it for?" indeed, implies a dim conception

beyond the "here" and the "now," a conception
which his stories should help him to clarify. If
we try to escape the pitfall of "fairy stories,"—
abandoning a child in unrealities,—we must not
fall into the opposite pitfall and continue the easy
habit of merely recounting a series of events,
neither significant in themselves nor, as in the
earlier years, significant because they are personal
experiences. "Arabella and Araminta" and their
like give a five-year-old no real food. They are
saved, if saved they are, not by their content, but
by a daring and skilful use of repetition and of
sound quality. No, our stories must add something to the children's knowledge and must take
them beyond the "here" and the "now." But this
"something," as I have already said, is not so much
new information as it is a new relationship among
already familiar facts.

In each of the stories for four- and five-year-olds
I have attempted to clarify known facts by showing them in a relationship a little beyond the children's own experience. All the stories came from
definite inquiries raised by some child. They attempt to answer these inquiries and to raise others.
"How the Engine Learned the Knowing Song,"
"The Fog Boat Story," "Hammer and Saw and
Plane," "How the Singing Water Gets to the

Tub," "Things That Loved the Lake," "The Children's New Dresses," "How Animals Move,"—all are based on definite relationships, largely physical, between simple physical facts.

Interest in these relationships,—inquiries which hold the germ of physical science, continue and increase with each year. In addition, a little later, children seem to begin questioning things social and to be ready for the simpler social relationships which underlie and determine the physical world of their acquaintance. "What's it for?" still dominates, but a six-year-old is on the way to becoming a conscious member of society. He now likes his answers to be in human terms. He takes readily to such conceptions as congestion as the cause for subways and elevated trains; the desire for speed as the cause of change in transportation; the dependence of man on other living things,— all of which I have made the bases of stories. To the children the material in "The Subway Car," "Speed," "Silly Will," is familiar; the relationships in which it appears are new.

Somewhere about seven years, there seems to be another transition period. Psychologists, whether in or out of schools, generally agree in this. Children of this age are acquiring a sense of social values,—a consciousness of *others* as sharply dis-

tinguished from themselves. They are also acquiring a sense of workmanship, of technique,—
of *things* as sharply distinguished from themselves. They seek information in and for itself,—
not merely in its immediate application to themselves. Their inquiries take on the character of
"how?" This means, does it not, that the children
have oriented themselves in their narrow personal
world and that they are reaching out for experience in larger fields? It means that the "not-me"
which was so shadowy in the earlier years has
gained in social and in physical significance. And
this again means that opportunity for exploration
in ever-widening circles should be given. Stories
should follow this general trend and open up the
relationships in larger and larger environments
until at last a child is capable of seeing relationships for himself and of regarding the whole world
in its infinite physical and social complexity, as his
own environment.

Probably the first extra-personal excursions
should be into alien scenes or experiences which
lead back or contribute directly to their old
familiar world. Stories of unknown raw material
which turn into well-known products are of this
type,—cattle raising in Texas, dairy farms in New
England, lumbering in Minnesota, sheep raising

in California. It is a happy coincidence that raw
materials are often produced under semi-primitive
conditions, so that a vicarious participation in their
production gives to children something of that
thrilling contact with the elemental that does the
life of primitive men, and this without sending
them into the remote and, for modern children,
"unnatural" world of unmodified nature. The
danger here is that the story will be sacrificed to
the information. Indeed it can hardly be otherwise, if the aim is to give an adequate picture of
some process of production. This, of course, is a
legitimate aim,—but for the encyclopedia, not for
the story. What I have in mind is a dramatic situation which has this process as a background,
so that the child becomes interested in the process
because of the part it plays in the drama just as he
would if the process were a background in his own
life. I am thinking of the opportunities which
these comparatively primitive situations give for
adventure rather than for the detailed elucidation
of a process of production.

It is the peculiar function of a story to raise
inquiries, not to give instruction. A story must
stimulate not merely inform. This is the trouble
with our "informational literature" for children,
of which very little is worthy of the name. In-

deed, I am not sure it is not a contradiction of
terms. It is frankly didactic. It aims to make
clear certain facts, not to stimulate thought. It
assumes that if a child swallows a fact it must
nourish him. To give the child material with
which to experiment,—this lies outside its present
range. Reaction from the unloveliness of this
didactic writing has produced a distressing result.
The misunderstood and misapplied educational
principle that children's work should interest them
has developed a new species of story,—a sort of
pseudo-literary thing in which the medicinal facts
are concealed by various sugar-coating devices.
Children will take this sort of story,—what will
their eager little minds not take? And like en-
cyclopedias and other books of reference this type
has its place in a child's world. But it should
never be confused with literature.

Literature must give a sense of adventure. This
sense of adventure, of excursion into the unknown,
must be furnished to children of every age. As I
have said before, I think "Peek-a-boo, there's the
baby!" is the elementary expression of this love
of adventure. The baby disappears into the unknown vastness behind the handkerchief and to
her, her reappearance is a thrilling experience.
Children's stories,—as indeed all stories,—have

been largely founded on this. The "Prudy" and "Dotty Dimple" books though keyed so low in the scale seem adventurous because of the meagre background of their young readers. But children of the age we are considering,—who have left the narrowly personal and predominantly play period demand something higher in the scale of adventure. To them are offered the great variety of tales of adventure and danger of which the boy scout is the latest example. Every child in reading these becomes a hero. And every child (and grown-up) enjoys being a hero. Higher still comes "Kidnapped" and so up to Stanley Weyman and "The Three Musketeers" which differ in their art, not in their appeal.

Now is it not possible to give children these adventurous excursions which they crave and should have, without so much killing of animals or men, and so many blood-thirsty excitements, and so much fake heroism? What relationships do such tales interpret? What truths do they give a child upon which to base his thinking? The relation of life to life is a delicate and difficult thing to interpret. But surely we can do better at an interpretation than tales of hunting, of impossible heroisms, and of war. Or at least, we can protest against having these almost the sole interpretations of adventure

which are offered to children. The world of industry holds possibilities for adventure as thrilling
as the world of high-colored romance. We must
look with fresh eyes to see it. When once we see
it, we shall be able to give the children a new type
of the "story of adventure." Of all the experiments which the stories in this collection repre-
sent, this attempt to find and picture the romance
and adventure in our world here and now, I con-
sider the most important and difficult. In such
stories as "Boris" and "Eben's Cows" and "The
Sky Scraper," I have made experimental attempts
to give children a sense of adventure by presenting social relations in this new way.

The cultured world has yet another answer to
the question, "How shall we give our children
adventure?" It points to the wealth of classical
myths, of Iliads, sagas, of fairy-stories which are
practically folk-lore, semi-magic, semi-allegorical,
semi-moral tales which express the ideals and experiences of a different and younger world than
ours of today. And it replies, "Give them these."
It feels in the sternness of saga stuff and in the
humanity of folk-lore, a validity and a dignity and
a simplicity which seem to make them suitable for
children. These tales tell of beliefs of folk less
experienced than we: we have outgrown them.

They must be suited to the less experienced: give them to children. Thus runs the common argument. And so we find Hawthorne's "Tanglewood Tales," Æsop's "Fables," various Indian myths and Celtic legends, and even the "Niebelungen Lied" often given to quite young children. But do we find this reasoning valid when we examine these tales free from the glamour which adult sophistication casts around them? Remember we are thinking now of children in that delicate seven- to eight-year-old transition period. I have already told how I believe these children are but just beginning to have conceptions of laws,—social and physical. They are groping their way, regimenting their experiences, seeing dim generalizations and abstractions. But they are not firmly oriented. They are beginners in the world of physical or social science and can be easily side-tracked or confused. A child of twelve or even ten is quite a different creature, often with clear if not articulate conceptions of the make-up of the physical and human world. He has something to measure against, some standards to cling to. But we are talking about children still in the early plastic stages of standards who will take the relationships we offer them through stories and build them into the very fabric of their thinking.

Now, how much of the classical literature follows the lead of the children's own inquiries? How much of it stimulates fruitful inquiries? What are the relationships which sagas, myths and folk-lore interpret? And what are the interpretations? This is a vast question and can be answered only briefly with the full consciousness that there is much lumping of dissimilar material with resulting injustices and superficiality. Also there is no attempt to use the words "myth," "saga" and "folk-lore" in technical senses.* I have merely taken the dominant characteristic of any piece of literature as determining its class.

Myths, properly, are slow-wrought beliefs which embody a people's effort to understand their relations to the great unknown. They are essentially religious, symbolic, mystic, subtle, full of fears and propitiations, involved, often based on the forgotten,—altogether unlike in their approach to the ingenuous and confident child. They are full of the struggle of life. Hardly before the involved introspections and theories of adolescence can we expect the real beauty and poignancy of a genuine myth to be even dimly understood. And

* For a clear exposition of this field of literature for children see "Literature in the Elementary School," by Porter Lander Mac-Clintock, University of Chicago Press, 1907.

why offer the shell without the spirit? It is likely
to remain a shell forever if we do. And indeed,
such an empty thing to most of us is the great myth
of Prometheus or of the Garden of Eden.

But sagas! Are they not of exactly the heroic
stuff for little children? In essence the relationships with which they deal are human,—social.
The story of Siegfried, of Achilles, of Abraham,—
these are great sagas. Each is a tremendous picture of a human experience, the first two under
heroic, enlarged conditions, the last under a human
culture picturesquely different from our own. But
even as straight tales of adventure they do not carry
for little children. The environment is too remote,
the world to be conquered too unknown to carry
a convincing sense of heroism to small children.
The same is true of the heroic tales of romance,—
of Arthur and all the legends which cluster around
his name. Magic, the children will get from these
tales but little else. But if the tales should succeed
in taking a child with them in their strange ex-
ploits into a strange land, they would surely fail to
take him into the turgid human drama they picture. And as surely we should wish them to fail.
The sagas, like most genuine folk-lore deal with
the great elemental human facts, life and death,
love, sexual passion and its consequences, mar-

riage, motherhood, fatherhood. We grasp at them
for our children, I believe, just *because* they deal
with these fundamental things,—the very things
we are afraid of unless they come to us concealed
in strange clothing. But what kind of a founda-
tion for interpreting these great elemental facts
will the stories of Achilles and Briseus, of Jason
and Medea, Pluto and Proserpina, of Guinevere
and Launcelot make? What do we expect a child
to get from these pictures of sexual passion on
the part of the man,—even though a god,—and
of social dependence of woman? Do Greek
draperies make prostitution suitable for children?
Does the glamour of chivalry explain illicit love?
Most parents and schools who unhesitatingly hand
over these social pictures to their children have
never tried,—and neither care nor dare to try,—
to face these elemental facts with their children.
Can we really wish to avoid a frank statement of
the *positive* in sex relations, of the facts of parent-
hood, of the institution of marriage, of the mutual
companionship between man and woman, and give
the *negative,* the unfulfilled, the distorted? This
is preposterous and no one would uphold it. It
must be the beauty of the tale, and not the significance we are after. But *are* these tales beautiful
except as we endow them with the subtleties of a

classical civilization, as we read into them piquant
contrasts of a sensitive, expressive race still primitive in its social thinking and social habits,—that
elusive thing which we mean by "Greek"? And
can children get this without its background, particularly as they have yet no social background
in their own world to hold it up against? And can
children do any better with the perplexing ideals
of the chivalrous knight swept by a human passion?

And in the same way can a child really get the
beauty of Siegfried? What can he make out of
the incestuous love of Siegmund and Sieglinda?
And of Siegfried's naïve passion on his first
glimpse of a woman? What do we want him to
make of it? Is that the way we wish to introduce
him to sex? And as for the rest, the allegory of the
ring itself, the sword, the dragon's blood, what do
little children get from this except the excitement
of magic? What *we* get because of what we have
to put into it, is a different matter and should never
be confused with the straight question of what children get. Outgrown adult thinking in social matters is no more suitable to children than outgrown
thinking on physical facts. We do not teach that
the world is flat because grown-ups once believed
it was. We are not afraid of a round earth so we

tell the truth about it. But we come near to teaching "spontaneous generation" with our endless evasions. We are afraid of a reproducing world, and so we fall back on curious mixtures of sex fables,—on storks and fairy godmothers and leave the mysteries of sex to be interpreted by Achilles and Siegfried and Guinevere! To emasculate these tales is to insult them,—to strip them of their significance and individuality. Is it not wiser to wait until children will not be confused by all their straight vigor and beauty?

There is other folk-lore less gripping in its human intensity. Through this may not children safely gain their needed adventures? And here we come again to the real "Märchen,"—the fairy tales. They take us into a lovely world of un-reality where magic and luck hold sway and where the child is safe from human problems and from scientific laws alike. I have already said in talking of the younger children that I feel it unsafe to loose a child in this unsubstantial world before he is fairly well grounded in a sense of reality. Once he has his bearings there is a good deal he will enjoy without confusion. The common de. fense that the mystery of fairy tales answers to a legitimate need in children, I believe holds good for children of six or seven, or even five, who have had opportunities for rational experiences. We all know how children revel in a secret. They like to live in a world of surprises. To give the children this sense of mystery I do not believe it is at all necessary to turn to vicious tales of giants, of ogres, and Bluebeards, or to the no less vicious pictures of the beautiful princess and the wicked stepmother. Even after rejecting the brutal and sentimental we have a good deal left,—a good deal that is intrinsically amusing as in "The Musicians of Bremen" or "Prudent Hans" or charming as in "Briar Rose." Symbolic or primitive attempts to explain the physical world,—as in the Indian legend of "Tavwots" I have never found held great appeal for the modern six- or seven-year-old scientists. Also the burden of symbolic morality rests on a good many of the traditional tales which usually neither adds nor detracts for the child and satisfies an adult yearning. Allegories like Æsop's "Fables" and "The Lion of Androcles" have a certain right to a hearing because of their historic prestige, apart from any reform they may accomplish in the way of character building. And in our own day many animals have achieved what I believe is a permanent place in child literature. "The Elephant's Child," the wild creatures of the "Jungle Book," "Raggylug" and even the little mole in the "Wind in the Willows,"—these are animals to trust any child with. Yet even in these exquisitely drawn tales, I doubt if children enjoy what we adults wish them to enjoy either in content or in form. And I doubt if we should accept even some of Kipling's matchless tales if the faultless form did not intrigue us and make us oblivious of the content.

It is just here that most of us fail to be discriminating. Most of the classical literature, most of the legends, or the folk tales that I have been discussing have a compelling charm through their form. But unfortunately that does not make their content suitable! Their place in the world's thinking and feeling and their transcription into their present forms by really great artists give them a permanent place in the world's literature. This I do not question. It is partly because I believe this so intensely that I wish them kept for fuller appreciation. It is as formative factors in a young child's thinking that I am afraid of them. Neither am I afraid of all of them. There are some old conceptions of life and death and human relations which the race has not outgrown, perhaps never will outgrow. The mystery and pathos of the Pied Piper, the humor of Prudent Hans, the cleverness of the boy David, the heroism of the little Dutch boy stopping the hole in the dyke, the love of the Queer Little Baker, and the greed and grief of Midas are eternal. In spite of these and many more, I maintain that for the most part, myths, sagas, folk-lore depend for their significance and beauty alike upon a grasp of present social values which a young child cannot have and that our first attention should be to give him those values in terms intelligible to him. After we have done that he is safe. It matters little what we give him so long as it is good: for he will have standards by which to judge our offerings for himself.

Yet after all is said and done, we may be reduced to giving children some of the stories we think inappropriate, for lack of something better. But a recognition of the need may evoke a great writer for children. I maintain we have never had one of the first order. The best books that we have for children are throw-offs from artists primarily concerned with adults,—Kipling and Stevenson stand in this group,—or child versions of adult literature,—from Charles and Mary Lamb down. The world has yet to see a genuinely great creator whose real vision is for children. When children have *their* Psalmist, *their* Shakespeare, *their* Keats, they will not be offered diluted adult literature.

So after we have gathered what we can from

the world's store for children of this seven-to-eight-year old period I think we shall find many unfilled gaps. Most attempts at humor, for instance, are on the level of the comic sheet of the Sunday supplement or the circus. There is little except a few of the "drolls" which give the child pure fun unmixed with excitement or confusion. Even "Alice in Wonderland" when first read to a six-year-old who was used to rational thinking and talking was pronounced "Too funny!" This same boy, however, went back to Alice again and again. He always relished such bits as:

"Speak roughly to your little boy,
  And beat him when he sneezes,
He only does it to annoy
  Because he knows it teases."

No child's world is complete without humor. And children have a sense of the preposterous, the inappropriate all their own. Lewis Carroll and a few others have occasionally found it. Still, I think much remains to be done in the way of studying the things that children themselves find amusing. This is true for the younger ones as well. I give several younger children's stories which appeared both to the tellers and their audiences to be convulsing. The humor is strangely physical and amazingly simple. And it is all fresh.

Stories by Four-Year-Olds

I dreamed I was asleep in a tomato and just scrambled around until I'd eaten it up.

Once there was a cow and he was in a wagon and he jumped over the wagon's edge.

Sesame the Cat

She lived with a nice man, a candy man, and she was at the gate watching the cattle go by and the men were digging under some caramel bricks and he called Sesame the Cat and she came banging and almost jumped on the man's head. She jumped like a merry balloon. Oh, he got angry!

Story by Five-Year-Old

Once there was a fly. And he went out walking on a little boy's face. He came to a kind of a soft hump. "What is this?" thought the fly. "Oh, I guess it's the little boy's eye!" Then he came to a lot of kind of wiggly things that went down with him. "What is this?" thought the fly. "Oh, I guess it's the little boy's hair!" Then he slipped and fell into a deep hole. It was the little boy's ear. And he couldn't get out. He tried and he tried. But he staid there until the little boy's ear got all sore!

Stories by Six-Year-Olds

Once upon a time there was a fox and a skunk, and the fox was walking down the path with a lot of prickly bushes on the side of the path. Then he saw a skunk coming along. He said, "Will you let me throw my little bag of perfume on you?" And then she (it was a lady fox) she backed and backed and backed and backed and backed and backed, and she backed so far she backed into the bushes, and she got her skirt torn on the prickly bushes.

Once upon a time there was a boy and the boy was awfully funny. And one day the boy went to the store to buy some eggs and he got the eggs and ran so fast with the eggs home,—he stumbled and broke the eggs. So he took the eggs, and took the shell and fixed it like the same egg. And he walked off slowly to his home. And his mother was going to beat the eggs and she just opened the shell and no egg was there, and she couldn't make no cake that night.

There is still another kind of story which I believe children of this transition period and a little older seek and for the most part seek in vain. These children are beginning to generalize, to marshal their facts and experiences along lines which in their later developments we call "laws." They like these wide-spreading conceptions which order the world for them. But they cannot always take them as bald scientific statements. Moreover there are certain general truths which tie together isolated familiar facts which can be most simply pictured through some device such as personification,—for at this age personification is recognized and enjoyed as a device and not, as in earlier years, as a necessary expression of thought. This uniting bond, this underlying relation may be a physical law like the dependence of life on life; it may be a social law like the division of labor in modern industry. Any dramatic statement of these laws is a simplification as is a diagram or map. And like a diagram or map, it is in a way artificial since it gives weight to one element at the expense of the others. But again like the diagram or map, the thing it shows is a fact, a fact which is more readily grasped by this artificial device than by bald statement. Maps do not take the place of photographs, nevertheless they have their own peculiar place in making ·intelligible the make-up of the physical world. In the same way, personification does not take the place of science. Nevertheless it has its own peculiar place in making clear to the child some simplifying principle,—physical or social,—which unifies his multitudinous experiences. So long as personification elucidates a true, a scientific principle, so long as it is not pressed to tortuous lengths which actually give false impressions, so long as it is kept within the bounds of æsthetic decency, so long as it is recognized as a play device and does not confuse a child's thinking,—so long it is justified. No more. It is a useful intellectual tool and a charming device for play. Kipling is preëminently the master here. It is a dangerous tool in lesser hands. Yet I have dared to use it and without scruple in "Speed," in "Once the Barn was Full of Hay" and in "Silly Will." Here again I feel sure that study of children's questions and stories would bring rich suggestions as to how to fill this large gap in their present literature.

Gaps there are, and many and large ones. Still, taken all in all, the field for the seven- to eight-year-old transition period is not as completely barren as the field for the earlier years. For these children are evolving from the stage where they need "Here and Now" stories. They are beginning to take on adult modes of thought and to appreciate and understand the peculiar language which adults use no matter how young a child they address! So much for the content of children's stories. And at best the content is but half.

FORM

If content is but half, form is the other half of stories and not the easier half, either. Every story, to be worthy of the name, must have a pattern, a pattern which is both pleasing and comprehensible. This design, this composition, this pattern, whether it be of a story as a whole or of a sentence or a phrase, is as essential to a piece of writing as is the design or composition to a picture. It satisfies the emotional need of the child which is as essential in real education as is the intellectual. Without this design, language remains on the utilitarian level,—where, to be sure, we usually find it in modern days.

Now what kind of pattern is adapted to a small child,—say a three-year-old? What kind does he like? More, what kind can he perceive? Here in the expression as fatally as in the content has the adult shaped the mould to his own liking. Or rather, the case is even worse. The adult more often than not has presented his stories and verse to children in forms which the children could not like because they literally could not hear them! The pattern, as such, did not exist for them. But what have we to guide us in creating suitable patterns for these little children who can help us neither by analysis nor by articulate remonstrance? We have two sources of help and both of them come straight from the children. The first are the children's own spontaneous art forms; the second are the story and verse patterns which make an

almost universal appeal to little children. Even
a superficial study of these two sources,—and
where shall we find a thorough study?—suggests
two fundamental principles. They sound obvious
and perhaps they are. But how often is the obvious
ignored in the treatment of children! The first
is that the individual units whether ideas, sentences or phrases must be simple. The second is
that these simple units must be put close together.

As the quickest and most eloquent exemplifica-
tion of both these principles I give four stories.
The first was told by a little girl of twenty-two
months, a singularly articulate little person,—as
she looked at the blank wall where had hung a
picture of a baby (she supposed her little brother),
a cow and a donkey. The second was a story told
by a little girl of two and a half after a summer
on the seashore. The third was achieved by a boy
of three,—a child, in general, unsensitive to music.
The fourth was told in school by a four-year-old
girl.

STORY BY TWENTY-TWO-MONTHS-OLD CHILD

> Where cow?
> Where donk?
> Where little Aa?

Cow gone away!
Donk gone away!
Little Aa gone away!

Like cow!
Like donk!
Like little Aa!

Come back cow!
Come back donk!
Come back little Aa!

STORY BY TWO-AND-A-HALF-YEAR-OLD

I fell in water.
Man fell in water.
John fell in water.
For' fell in water.
Aunt Carrie fell in water.

I pull boat out.
Man pull boat out.
John pull boat out.
For' pull boat out.
Aunt Carrie pull boat out.

I go in that boat.
Man go in that boat.
John go in that boat.
For' go in that boat.
Aunt Carrie go in that boat.

STORY BY THREE-YEAR-OLD

And father went down, down, down into the hole.
And the bull-frog, he went up, up, up into the sky!
And then the bull-frog, he went down, down, down into
    the hole
And then father, he went up, up, up, way into the sky!
And then the bull-frog he went down, down, down into
    the hole
And up, up into the sky!
And then he went down into the hole
And up into the sky!
And he went down and up and down and up
And down and up and down and up
And down and up and down and up
And down and up
And down and up
And down and up
Down and up————————(to wordless song.)

STORY BY A FOUR-YEAR-OLD

Baby Bye, Baby Bye
Here's a fly
You'd better be careful
Else he will sting you
And here's a spider too.
And if you hurt him he will sting you
And don't you hurt him
And his pattern on the wall.

Certainly all have form,—spontaneous native art
form. Indeed they strongly suggest that to the

child, the pleasure lay in the form rather than in
the content. The patterns of the first two are somewhat alike,—variations of a simple statement. In
content the younger child keeps her attention on
one point, so to speak, while the older child allows
a slight movement like an embryonic narrative.
The pattern of the three-year-old's is considerably
more complex. The phrases shorten, the tempo
quickens, until the whole swings off into wordless
melody. The fourth probably started from some
remembered lullaby but quickly became the child's
own. I give two more examples of stories. In the
first, does not this five-year-old girl give us her
vivid impressions in marvelously simple sense and
motor terms? And does not the six-year-old boy
in the second show that imagination can spring
from real experiences?

Stories by Five-Year-Olds

I am going to tell you a story about when I went
to Falmouth with my mother. We had to go all night
on the train and this is the way it sounded, (moving
her hand on the table and intoning in different keys)
thum, thum, thum, thum, thum, thum, thum, thum,
NEWARK! thum, thum, thum, thum, thum, thum,
thum, thum, thum, thum, FALMOUTH! And then
we got off and we took a trolley car and the trolley
car went clipperty, clipperty, clipperty, zip, zip. And

another trolley car came in the other direction (again with hands) and one came along saying clipperty, clipperty, clipperty, zip, zip and the other came along saying clipperty, clipperty, clipperty, zip, zip, zip, BANG! And they hit in the middle and they got stuck and they tried to pull them apart and they stuck and they stuck and they stuck and finally they got them apart and then we went again. And when we got off we had to take a subway and the subway went rockety-rockety-rockety-rock. You know a subway makes a terrible noise! It made a *terrible* noise it sounded like rockety-rockety-rockety-rockety-rock.

And at last we got there and when we came up in the streets of Falmouth it was so still that I didn't know what to do. You know the streets of Falmouth are just so terribly quiet and then we had to walk millions and millions of miles almost to get to our little cottage. And when we got there I put on my bathing suit and I went in bathing and I shivered just like this because it was a rainy day, the day I went to Falmouth with my mother.

The Talk of the Brook

O brook, O brook, that sings so loud,
O brook, O brook, that goes all day,
O brook, O brook, that goes all night
And forever.
Splashes and waves, girls and boys are playing with
You and in you.
Some with shoes off and some with shoes on,
And some are crying because they fell in you.
O brook, O brook, have you an end ever?
Or do you go forever?

Technically in all these stories the child exempli-
fies the two rules. He attends to but one thing at
a time. And his steps from one point to the next
are short and clear.

When we look at the forms which have been
presented to children with these their spontaneous
patterns fresh in mind, we can see, I think, why
Mother Goose has been taken as a child's own and
Eugene Field and even Stevenson rejected as unin-
telligible. I do not believe there is anything in the
content of Mother Goose to win the child. I
believe it is the form that makes the appeal.
Vachel Lindsay, whose daring play with words
has made him an object of suspicion to the reluc-
tant of mind, has given us one poem in pattern
singularly like the children's own and in content
full of interest and charm. Again I give examples
as the quickest of arguments. And I give them in
verse where the form is more obvious and can be
shown in briefer space than in stories.

> Jack and Jill
> Went up the hill
> To fetch a pail of water.
> Jack fell down
> And broke his crown
> And Jill came tumbling after.

TIME TO RISE

A birdie with a yellow bill
Hopped upon the window sill,
Cocked his shining eye and said:
"Ain't you shamed, you sleepy head?"

—*Stevenson.*

THE LITTLE TURTLE

(A recitation for Martha Wakefield, three years old)

There was a little turtle.
He lived in a box.
He swam in a puddle.
He climbed on the rocks.

He snapped at a musquito.
He snapped at a flea.
He snapped at a minnow.
And he snapped at me.

He caught the musquito.
He caught the flea.
He caught the minnow.
But he didn't catch me.

—*Vachel Lindsay.*

From THE DINKEY-BIRD

So when the children shout and scamper
    And make merry all the day,
When there's naught to put a damper
    To the ardor of their play;

When I hear their laughter ringing,
Then I'm sure as sure can be
That the Dinkey-bird is singing
In the amfalula tree.
                        —*Eugene Field.*

Of the two "Jack and Jill" and "Birdie with the
Yellow Bill," surely Stevenson's is the more
charming to the adult ear. But when I have read
it to three-year-olds, I have felt that they were
lost. They could not sustain the long grammatical
suspense, could not carry over "A birdie" from the
first line to the conclusion and so actually did not
know who was saying "Ain't you shamed, you
sleepy-head!" Mother Goose repeats her subject.
The span to carry is two phrases in Mother Goose
as against four in Stevenson. The Vachel Lindsay
I have found is as easily remembered and as much
enjoyed as Mother Goose, though it is a pity it is
about an unfamiliar animal. As for the Dinkey-
bird even a seven-year-old can hardly *hear* the
rhyme even if intellectually he could follow the
adult vocabulary and the complicated sentence
with its long postponed subject.

It is the same with stories. The classic tales
which have held small children,—"The Gingerbread Man," "The Three Little Pigs," "Goldy-
locks,"—have patterns so obvious and so simple

that they cannot be missed. In "The Gingerbread Man" the pattern is one of increasing additions. It belongs to the aptly called "cumulative" tales. The refrains act like sign-posts to help the child to mark the progress. This is simply a skilful way of making the continuity close, of showing the ladder rungs for the child's feet. I venture to say that any good story-teller consciously or unconsciously puts up sign-posts to help the children. If he is skilful, he makes a pattern of them so that they are not merely intellectually helpful but charming as well. So Kipling in his "Just So Stories" uses his sign-posts,—which are sometimes words, sometimes phrases, sometimes situations,— in such a way that they ring musically and give a pleasant sense of pattern even to children too young to find them intellectually helpful.

In other words, the little child is not equipped psychologically to hear complicated units. I wish some one could determine how the average four-year-old hears the harmony of a chord on the piano. Is it much except confusion? In the same way, he is not equipped to leap a span between units. I wish some one would determine the four-year-old's memory span for rhymes, for instance. The involutions, the suggestiveness so attractive to adult ears, he cannot hear. Even an adult ear, untutored, can scarcely hear the intermingling rhythms and overlapping rhymes which blend like overtones of a chord in such verse as Patmore's Ode "The Toys." I feel sure the small child cannot hear complexities; he cannot leap gaps. And so he cannot understand when even simple ideas are given in complex and discontinuous form. This explains his notorious love of repetition. Repetition is the simplest of patterns, simple enough to be enjoyed as pattern. I have found that almost any simple phrase of music or words repeated slowly and with a kind of ceremonious attention, enthralls a year-old child. If the unit is simple enough to be remembered he will inevitably enjoy recognizing it as it recurs and recurs. This is the embryonic pattern sense.

This pattern enjoyment too is motor in its basis. His early repetitions of sounds are probably largely pleasure in muscle patterns. We all know that a child uses first his large muscles,—arm, leg and back,—and that he early enjoys any regular recurrent use of these muscles. So at the time when the vocal muscles tend to become his means of expression, he enjoys repeating the same sounds over and over. And soon he gets enjoyment from listening to repetitions or rhythmic language,—a vicarious motor enjoyment. Surely it is important that stories should furnish him this exercise and pleasure. Three- and four-year-olds will enjoy a positively astounding amount of repetition. In the Arabella and Araminta stories a large proportion of the sentences are given in duplicate by the simple device of having twins who do and say the same things and by telling the remarks and actions of each. The selection quoted is repeated entire four times, the variation being only in the flower picked:

And Arabella picked a poppy, and Araminta picked a poppy, and Arabella picked a poppy, and Araminta picked a poppy, and Arabella picked a poppy, and Araminta picked a poppy, and Arabella picked a poppy, and Araminta picked a poppy, and Arabella picked a poppy, and Araminta picked a poppy, until they each had a great big bunch (I should say a very large bunch), and then they ran back to the house.

Arabella got a glass and put her poppies in it, and Araminta got a glass and put her poppies in it.

And Arabella clapped her hands and danced around the table. And Araminta clapped her hands and danced around the table.

Adult ears repudiate anything as obvious as this; they still, however, enjoy a ballad refrain.

Just as small children cannot hear complications, so they cannot grasp details if the movement is swift. We must give time for a child's slow reactions. We usually fail to do this in ordinary social situations and are often surprised to hear our three-year-old say "good-bye" long after the front door is closed and our guest well on his way down the street. In stories we must take a leisurely pace. We must also read very slowly allowing ample time for a child to give the full motor expression to his thought for the art of abbreviation he has not yet learned.

It is not enough to recognize that since a child attends to but one thing at a time the units must be simple. Here in the form as in the content, must the motor quality of a child's thinking be held constantly in mind. In trying to find the general subject matter appropriate for little children I said that they think through their muscles. This motor expression of small children has its direct application in the concrete method of telling of any happening. The story child who is experiencing, should go through the essential muscular performances which the real listening child would go through if he were actually experiencing himself. For he thinks through these muscular expressions. As an example, when a group of four-year-olds heard a story about a little boy who saw the elevated train approach and pass above him, they thought the child might have been run over. The words "up" and "above" and "overhead" had been used but the children failed to get the idea of "upness." Unquestionably they would have understood if I had made the little boy *throw back his head and look up*. Small children act with big gestures and with big muscles. And they think through the same mechanisms.

These two principles, simplicity and continuity, apply concretely to sentence and phrase structure as well. The effort to obtain continuity for the child explains the colloquial "The little boy who lived in this house, *he* did so and so——" You help your child back to the subject, "the little boy" by the grammatically redundant "he" after his mind has gone off on "this house." This same need for continuity also explains why a child's own stories are characteristically one continuous sentence strung together with "ands" and "thens" and "buts." He sees and hears and consequently thinks in a simple, rhythmic, continuous flow. If we would have him see and hear and think with us, we must give him his stories and verse in simple units closely and obviously linked together.

But after all is said and done, why should we give children stories at all? Is it to instruct and so should we pay attention to the content? Is it to delight and so should we pay attention to the form? Both things, information and relish, have their place in justifying stories for children. But both to my mind are of minor importance compared to a third and quite different thing,—and this is to get children to create stories of their own, to play with words. "To get" is an unhappy phrase for it suggests that children must be coaxed to the task. This I do not believe though I cannot prove it. I do believe that children play with words naturally and spontaneously just as they play with any material that comes to their creative hands. And further I believe,—though this too I cannot prove,—that we adults kill this play with words just as we kill their creative play with most things. Most of us have forgotten how to play with anything, most of all with words. We are utilitarian, we are executive, we are didactic, we are earth-tied, we are hopelessly adult! Actually children use their ears and noses and fingers much more than do we adults. Our stories rely mainly upon visual recalls. We forget to listen even to birds whose message is pure melody. And how many of us *hear* the city sounds which surround us, the characteristic whirr of revolving wheels, the vibrating rhythm of horses' feet, the crunch of footsteps in the snow? Noises we hear, the warning shriek of the fire engine or the honk! honk! of

the automobile. But the subtler, finer reverbera-
tions we are not sensitive to. Yet little children
love to listen and develop another method of sens-
ing and appreciating their world by this pleasurable use of their hearing. It surely is an unused
opportunity for story-tellers. I have tried to use
it in "Pedro's Feet" which is an attempt to give
them an ordinary story by means of sounds. And
even less than to city sounds do we listen for the
cadences in language. We listen only for the
meaning and forget the sensuous delight of sound.

But happily children are not so determined to
wring a meaning out of every sight and every
sound. Children play. Play is a child's own technique. Through it he seizes the strange unknown
world around him and fashions it into his very
own. He recreates through play. And through
creating, he learns and he enjoys.

There is no better play material in the world
than words. They surround us, go with us through
our work-a-day tasks, their sound is always in our
ears, their rhythms on our tongue. Why do we
leave it to special occasions and to special people
to use these common things as precious play material? Because we are grown-ups and have closed
our ears and our eyes that we may not be distracted
from our plodding ways! But when we turn to the

children, to hearing and seeing children, to whom
all the world is as play material, who think and
feel through play, can we not then drop our adult
utilitarian speech and listen and watch for the patterns of words and ideas? Can we not care for
the *way* we say things to them and not merely *what*
we say? Can we not speak in rhythm, in pleasing
sounds, even in song for the mere sensuous delight
it gives us and them, even though it adds nothing
to the content of our remark? If we can, I feel
sure children will not lose their native use of
words: more, I think those of six and seven and
eight who have lost it in part,—and their stories
show they have,—will win back to their spontaneous joy in the play of words. This is the ultimate
test of stories and verse,—whether they help children to retain their native gift of play with language and with thought.

In the City and Country School where my experiments in language have been carried on, we
have not gone far enough to offer convincing proof
along these lines. But I submit two stories told
by a six-year-old class which are at least sugges-
tive. The first is the best story told to me by any
member of the class before any effort had been
made to get the children to listen to the sound of
their words or to think of their ideas as all point-

ing in one direction and giving a single impression. The second was told by the class as a whole while looking at Willebeek Le Mair's illustration of "Twinkle, twinkle, little star." They said the picture made them feel sleepy and that they would say only things that made them sleepy and use only words that made them sleepy. Between the two stories I had met with them seven times. I had read them sounding and rhythmic verse. They had become interested in the sound of language apart from its meaning. They had become interested in the sound of the rain and the fire. They were thinking through their ears. Am I mistaken in believing this shows in their language and in their thought?

Story by a Six-Year-Old

Once upon a time there was a little boy named Peter and a little boy named Boris. And Peter took him out for a walk and took him all around school. Then I took him out to my house and saw all my play things. And then I took him to Central Park and showed him sea lions and the giraffe and the elephant and I showed how they eat by their trunks. And he thought it was queer. And he said he was afraid of animals and so I took him home. I told him to tell his mother about it and his mother said, "You want to go for another walk?" and he said, "Yes, but not where the wild animals are." I said, "Do you want to go to Central Park?" and he said, "Yes." You see he got fooled! He didn't know about the wild animals.

JOINT STORY BY SIX-YEAR-OLD CLASS

I like it when the boy and the girl look at the sky. They look at the trees and they are sleepy. It is dark outside. It is night and the sky is dark blue. And it is kind of whitish and the trees are next to the blue sky. The bright evening star is out. The star is so far up in the sky that you can hardly see it. The children are looking at the sky before they go to bed and they are praying to God. They have their nightgowns on. The bed is all nice so they couldn't have just got up. The clothes are hanging on the bed. They sleep in their own bed together. When they go to bed they have their door closed.

"The Leaf Story" and "The Wind Story" I have incorporated with my stories, though they are almost entirely the work of children. In both cases the organization is beyond the children. But the content and the phraseology bear their unmistakable imprint. The same is true of "The Sea Gull."

Because of the pattern, the play aspect of language, I believe in written stories even for very little ones. If we loved our language better and played with its sound in our ordinary speech, perhaps stories for two- and three-year-olds would not be needed. But as it is, we need to present them

with something more intentional, more thought out
than is possible with most of us in a story told.
If the patterns of our ideas or of our speech are
to have charm, if they are to fit the occasion with
nicety, if they are to flow easily and are to be continuous enough to be comprehended by little children, they will need careful attention,—attention
that cannot be given under the emergency of telling a story, not, at least, by the uninspired of us.
Inevitably, with our utilitarian tendencies, we
shall be drawn off to an undue regard of the content to the neglect of the expression. And yet,
for very little children, there is unquestionably
something lost by the formality and fixity of a
written story. A story told has more spontaneity,
allows more leeway to include the chance happenings or remarks of the children; it can be more
intimately personal, more adapted to the particular occasion and to the particular child. Perhaps
some time we shall achieve a fortunate com-
promise, a stepping stone between the story told
and the story read. Perhaps we shall work out
happy or characteristic phrases about familiar
things,—little personal things about the clothes and
habits of each child, general familiar things like
autos and wagons and horses on the street, coal
going down the hole in the sidewalk, the squab-

bling of sparrows in the dirt, the drift of snow on
the roofs,—perhaps we shall learn to use such
thought-out phrases or refrains like blocks for
building many stories. If we could work out some
such technique as this, we could keep the intimacy,
the flexibility, the waywardness of the spoken
story and still give the children the charm of careful thinking and careful phrasing. Many such
phrases have been fashioned by people sensitive
to the quality of sound. Every nursery has had
its rooster crow:

"Cock-a-doodle-doo!"

But few have given its children that delightful
epitome of the songs of spring birds which has
piped with irrepressible freshness now for nearly
four centuries:

"Cuckoo, jug-jug, pu-we, to-witta-woo!"

I have never known the child who did not respond
to Kipling's engine song:

"With a michnai-ghignai-shtingal! Yah! Yah! Yah!"

Every child creates these wonderful sound interpretations of the world. We smile a smile of in-
dulgence when we hear them. And then we forget

them! Cannot we seize some of them however imperfectly and learn to build them into the structure of our stories? It was more or less this kind of thing that I had in mind in writing Marni's stories and "The Room with the Window Looking Out Upon the Garden" which as I have said elsewhere are types to be told rather than narratives to be read. And I feel sure if we could once make a beginning that the children themselves would soon take the matter into their own hands and create their own building blocks.

For children are primarily creators. They do not willingly nor for long maintain the passive rôle. This should be reckoned with in stories and not merely as a concession to restless children but as a real aid to the story. An active rôle should be provided for the children somewhere within every story until the children are old enough to have a genuinely impersonal interest in things and events and until they do not need a motor expression of their thoughts. For as I have already said, up to that age,—and it is for psychologists to say when that age is,—children think in terms of themselves expressed through their own activities. This active rôle should be used not merely as a safety valve of expression to keep the child a patient listener, but as a tool by which he may become aware of the form of thought and language. It is interesting that the children to whom these stories have been read, have seized upon the rhyme refrains as their own and after a few readings have joined in saying them as though this were their natural portion. It is with this hope that I have tried to make the refrains not mere interludes in the story, as they usually are, but the real skeleton, the intrinsic thought pattern, the fundamental design. In "How the Singing Water Gets to the Tub" and "How Spot Found a Home," for instance, the refrains taken by themselves out of the context, tell the whole story. It is too soon to say, but I am strong in the hope that through relish for this kind of active participation in written stories, a small child may become captivated by the play side of the stories as opposed to the content and so turn to language as play material in which to fashion patterns of his own.

For the sake of analysis, I have treated content and form separately. But I am keenly aware that the divorce of the two is what has made our stories for children so unsatisfactory. We have good ideas told without charm of design; and we have meaningless patterns which tickle the ear for the moment but fade because they spring from no real thought. Literature is only achieved when the

thought pattern and the language pattern exactly
fit. A refrain for the mere sake of recurrent
jingle, that has no genuine no essential recurrence
in the thought, is a trick. If the pattern does not
help the thought and the thought suggest the pattern, there is something wrong. It is an artifice,
not art. This matching of content and form is
nothing new. It is and always has been the basis
of good literature. The task that is new is to find
thought sequences, thought relations which are
truly childlike and the language design which is
really appropriate to them,—to make both content
and form the child's.

As I said at the beginning, so must I say at the
end. These stories are experiments, experiments
both in content and form. To have any value they
must be treated as such. The theses underlying
them have been stated for brevity's sake only in
didactic form. In reality, they lie in my mind
as open questions urgently in need of answers. But
I do not hope much from the answers of adults,—
from the deaf and blind writers to the hearing and
seeing children. The answers must come from
the children themselves. We must listen to children's speech, to their casual everyday expressions.
We must gather children's stories. Mothers and
teachers everywhere should be making these

precious records. We must study them not merely as showing what a child is thinking, but the *way* he is thinking and the way he is enjoying. It is the hope that these stories may be tried out with children, the hope of reaching others who may be watching and listening and working along these lines, the hope that we may gather records of children's stories which will become a basis for a real literature, the hope that somewhere among grownups we may find an ear still sensitive to hear and an eye still fresh to see,—it is this hope that has given me the courage to expose these pitifully inadequate adult efforts to speak with little children in their own language. Some one must dare, if only to give courage to the better equipped. And if we dare enough, I am sure the children will come to our rescue. If we let them, they will lead us. Whatever these stories hold of merit or of suggestiveness is due to the inspiration and tolerance of the courageous group of workers in the City and Country School and in the Bureau of Educational Experiments and in particular to Caroline Pratt without whom these stories would never have been dreamed or written; and above all to the children themselves, for whom the stories were written and to whom they have been read, both in the laboratory school and in my own home.

To those then, who wish to follow the lead of little children, to those who have the curiosity to know into what new paths of literature children's interest and children's spontaneous expression of those interests will lead, and to the children themselves, I send these stories.

LUCY SPRAGUE MITCHELL.

New York City
July, 1921.

MARNI TAKES A RIDE
IN A WAGON

The refrains in this story were first made up during the actual ride. Later they served to recall the experience with vividness. This story is given only as a type which any one may use when helping a two-year-old to live over an experience.

MARNI TAKES A RIDE IN A WAGON

One day Marni went for a ride. Little Aa, he climbed into Sprague's wagon and Marni, she climbed in behind him. Then Mother took the handle and she began to pull the wagon with little Aa and Marni in it. And Mother she went:

Jog, jog, jog, jog,
Jog, jog, jog, jog,
Jog, jog, jog, jog,
Jog, jog, jog, jog,
And Jog, jog, jog, jog,
Jog, jog, jog, jog,
Jog, jog, jog, jog,
Jog!

And the wheels, they went, (with motion of hands) :

Round, round, round, round,
Round, round, round, round,
Round, round, round, round,
Round, round, round, round,
And Round, round, round, round,
Round, round, round, round,
Round, round, round, round,
Round!

And then Mother was tired. So she stopped. And Marni said, "Whoa, horsie!"

Then Little Aa said, "Ugh, ugh!" for he wanted
to go.

But Marni said, "Get up, horsie!" for she
wanted to go too. So Mother took hold of the
handle and went:

Jog, jog, jog, jog,
Jog, jog, jog, jog,
Jog, jog, jog, jog,
Jog, jog, jog, jog,
And Jog, jog, jog, jog,
Jog, jog, jog, jog,
Jog, jog, jog, jog,
Jog!

And the wheels they went:

Round, round, round, round,
Round, round, round, round,
Round, round, round, round,
Round, round, round, round,
And Round, round, round, round,
Round, round, round, round,
Round, round, round, round,
Round!

And then Mother was tired. So she stopped.
and Marni said, "Whoa, horsie!"

Then Little Aa said, "Ugh, ugh!" for he wanted
to go. But Marni said "Get up, horsie!" for she
wanted to go too. So Mother took hold of the
handle and went,

> Jog, jog, jog, jog,
> Jog, jog, jog, jog,
> Jog, jog, jog, jog,
> Jog, jog, jog, jog,
> *And* Jog, jog, jog, jog,
> Jog, jog, jog, jog,
> Jog, jog, jog, jog,
> Jog!

And the wheels they went:

> Round, round, round, round,
> Round, round, round, round,
> Round, round, round, round,
> Round, round, round, round,
> *And* Round, round, round, round,
> Round, round, round, round,
> Round, round, round, round,
> Round!

And then Mother was very, *very* tired. So she stopped. And Marni said, "Whoa, horsie!"

Then Little Aa said, "Ugh, ugh!" for he wanted to go again. But Marni said "Get up, horsie!" for she wanted to go too. But Mother she was very, *very,* VERY tired. She had jogged, jogged, jogged so long and made the wheels go round, round, round, round, so much! So she said, "The ride is all over!" Then Little Aa climbed down out of the wagon and Marni climbed down out of the wagon. And Marni said, "Goodbye, wagon!" and ran away!

MARNI GETS DRESSED
IN THE MORNING

This story, obviously, is for a particular little girl. It is told in the terms of her own experience, of her own environment, and of her own observations. It is nothing more or less than the living over in rhythmic form of the daily routine of her morning dressing. Her story remarks are either literal quotations or adaptations of her actual every day responses. The little verse refrains are the type of thing almost anyone can improvise. I have found that any simple statement about a familiar object or act told (or sung) with a kind of ceremonious attention and with an obvious and simple rhythm, enthralls a two-year-old. The little girl for whom this story was written began embryonic stories before her second birthday. The water-soap-sponge episode is an adaptation of one of her first narrative forms. This story is meant merely as a suggestion of the way almost anyone can make language an every day plaything to the small child she is caring for.

MARNI GETS DRESSED IN THE MORNING

Once there was a little girl and her name was Marni Moo. Marni used to sleep in a little bed in mother's room. In the morning Marni would wake up and she would say "Hello, Mother." And then in a minute she would say, "I want to get up."

And mother would say:

"Hoohoo, Marni Moo.
I'm coming, I'm coming,
I'm coming for you."

Then mother would get up and she'd come over and she'd unfasten the blanket and she'd take little Marni Moo in her arms and she'd walk into Marni's bath-room and she'd take off Marni's night-gown and Marni's shirt. And then she'd get a little basin, and she'd put some water in it, and she'd get some soap and she'd get a sponge and she'd wash little Marni Moo. She'd wash Marni's face and then she'd wash Marni's hands, and Marni would put one hand in the basin and she'd splash

the water like this:—   Then she'd put
another hand in the basin and she'd splash the
water like this:—   Then mother would
wipe both hands and she'd throw the water down
the sink and she'd put away the soap and the
sponge.   And Marni would watch mother and
then she'd say:

"Where water?
Where soap?
Where sponge?

> Water gone away!
> Soap gone away!
> Sponge gone away!"

And after that what do you suppose Marni would say?

"Shirt, shirt." And mother would put Marni's shirt over her head and say:

> "Peek-a-boo, Marni Moo,
> Marni's head is coming through."

and then mother would button up Marni's shirt.

And then Marni would say "Waist, waist." Then while mother put on Marni's waist she would say:

> "Here's one hand
> And here's another.
> Marni's a sister
> And Robin's a brother."

And then Marni would say, "Drawers, drawers." And while mother put on Marni's drawers she would say:

> "Here's one foot
> And here's another.
> Marni's a sister
> And Peter's a brother."

And then Marni would say, "Stockings, stockings." And mother would put on one stocking on her left foot, and then she'd put on another stocking on her right foot. And then she'd fasten the garters on one stocking, and then she'd fasten the garters on the other stocking. And all the time mother would keep saying:

> "Here's one leg
> And here's another.
> Marni's a sister
> And Jack-o's a brother."

Then Marni would say, "Shoe, shoe." And mother would put one shoe on her left foot and then she'd put on the other shoe on her right foot. And then she'd say again:

> "Here's one foot
> And here's another.
> Marni's a sister
> And Robin's a brother."

And then Marni would say, "Hook, hook." And mother would get the button-hook and then she'd button up the left shoe and then she'd button up the right shoe. And all the time she was buttoning up first one shoe and then the other shoe Marni would say:

> "Look, look,
> Hook, hook."

And when the shoes were all buttoned up, mother
would hit first one little sole and then the other
little sole, and say:

> "Now we're through
> Tit, tat, too.
> Here a nail, there a nail,
> Now we're through."

Then Marni would run and get her romper and
bring it to mother calling, "Romper, romper."
And mother would put on her romper, singing:

> "Romper, romper
> Who's got a romper?
> Little Marni Moo
> She's got two.
> One is a yellow one
> And one is blue.
> Romper, romper
> Who's got a romper?"

And then Marni would say, "Button, button."
And mother would button up her romper all
down the back. First one button and then another
button and then another button and then another
button, and then another button and then another
button until they were buttoned all down the back.

And then Marni would say, "Sweater." And
mother would put on her little blue sweater saying:

"Sweater, sweater
Who's got a sweater?
Little Marni Moo
She's got two.
One is a yellow one
And one is blue.
Sweater, sweater,
Who's got a sweater?"

And then Marni would say, "Hair." And
mother would get the brush and comb and brush
Marni's hair. And all the time she was brushing
it she would say:

"Brush it so
And brush it slow.
Brush it here
And brush it there.
Brush it so
And brush it slow.
And brush it here
And brush it there
And brush it all over your dear little head."

And then Marni would say, "All ready." And
mother would put her down on the floor.
Then Marni would say:

"Where my little pail?
My little pail gone away.
I want my little pail
Come, little pail."

And mother would give her her little pail. And Marni would put one nut in her pail, and then she'd put another nut in her pail, and then she'd put another nut in her pail. And then she'd put a marble in her pail, and then she'd put another marble in her pail, and then she'd put another marble in her pail. And then she'd put her quack-quack in her pail, and then she'd put her fish in her pail, and then she'd put her frog in her pail. Then she would shake her pail with all of the nuts and the marbles and the quack-quack and the frog and the fish, and they would all go bingety-bang, crickety-crack, bingety-bang, crickety-crack.

And Marni would say, "Bingety-bang, crickety-crack. Where Jack-o?" And Marni would run to find Jack-o, and she would say, "Jack-o, hear bingety-bang, crickety-crack." And she would rattle her little pail with all the nuts and the marbles and the quack-quack and the fish and the frog. Then she'd say, "Where Peter?" And Marni would run to find Peter, and she would say, "Peter, hear bingety-bang, crickety-crack." And she would rattle her little pail with all the nuts and the marbles and the quack-quack and the fish and the frog.

Then mother would call, "Breakfast, breakfast. Anyone ready for breakfast?"

And Jack-o would call back, "I am, I am, I am ready for breakfast."

And Peter would run as fast as he could calling, "I am, I am, I am ready for breakfast."

And last of all would come little Marni Moo calling, "Breakfast, breakfast."

Then the two boys would chase Marni to the breakfast table saying:

> "Marni Mitchell,
> Marni Moo,
> Run like a mousie
> Or I'll catch you."

And Marni would scimper scamper like a mousie until she reached the breakfast table.

Then they would all have breakfast together.

THE ROOM WITH THE
WINDOW LOOKING OUT
ON THE GARDEN

In this story written for a three-year-old group, I have tried to present the familiar setting of the classroom from a new point of view and to give the presentation a very obvious pattern. I want the children to take an *active* part in the story. But before they try to do this I want them to have some conception of the whole pattern of the story so that their contributions may be in proper design, both in substance and in length. That is the reason I give two samples before throwing the story open to the children. If each child has a part which falls into a recognized scheme, through performing that part he gets a certain practice in pattern making in language,—however primitive— and also a certain practice in the technique of co-operation which means listening to the others as well as performing himself. I have not tried to add anything to their stock of information,—merely to give them the pleasure of drawing on a common fund together.

THE ROOM WITH THE WINDOW LOOK-
ING OUT ON THE GARDEN

Once there was a little girl. She was just three
years old. One morning she and her mother put
on their hats and coats right after breakfast. They
walked and walked and walked from their house
until they came to MacDougal Alley. And then
they walked straight down the alley into the Play
School. Now the little girl had never been to the
Play School before and she didn't know where
anything was and she didn't know any of the children and she didn't even know her teacher! So
she asked her mother, "Which room is going to
be mine?" And her mother answered, "The one
with the window looking out on the garden."

And sure enough, when the little girl looked
around there was the sun shining right in through
a window which looked out on a lovely garden!
She knelt right down on the window sill to look
out.

Then she heard some one say, "Little New Girl,
why don't you take off your things?" She turned
around and there was Virginia talking to her.

"Because I don't know where to put them," said Little New Girl. "How funny!" laughed Virginia, "because see, here are all the hooks right in plain

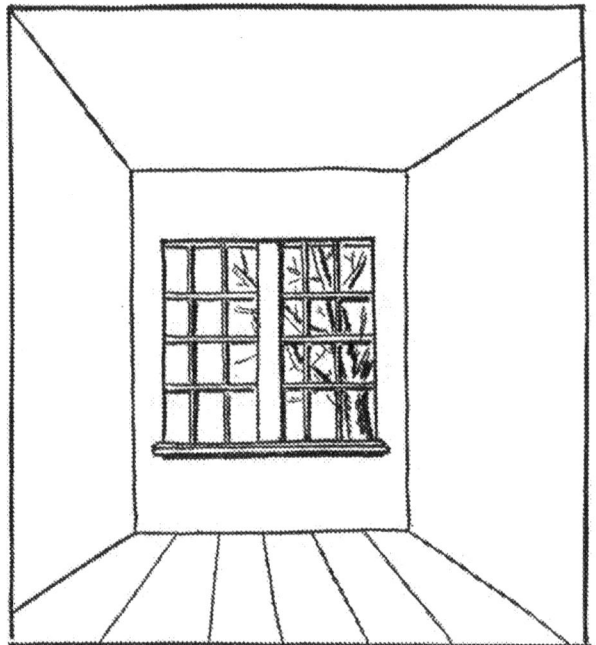

sight," and she pointed under the stairs. So the little girl took off her hat and her mittens. Her mother had to unbutton the hard top button but she did all the rest. Then she hung up everything on a hook.

"Goodbye," said her mother. "Goodbye," said Little New Girl. "Don't forget to come for me because I don't know where anything is and I don't know the children and I don't even know my teacher." And her mother answered, "No, I won't." And then she was gone.

"Now, Little New Girl, what do you want to do?" said her teacher. But the little girl only shook her head and said, "I don't know anything to do." One little boy said, "Let me show Little New Girl something." And what did he show her? He took her over to the shelves and he showed her the blocks. "You can build a house or anything with them," said the little boy.

Then another little girl said, "Let me show Little New Girl something." And what did this other little girl show her? She showed her the dolls. "You can put them into a house," said this other little girl.

"Who else can show Little New Girl something to do?" called her teacher. "Will you, Robert?" So what did Robert show her? (Give child ample time to think. If he does not respond go on.) Robert took her over to the shelves and showed her the paper and crayons. "You can draw ever so many pictures," said Robert.

Then Virginia said, "Let me show Little New

Girl something." So what did Virginia show her?
—Virginia showed her the horses and wagons.
"You can harness them up," said Virginia.

Then Craig said, "Let *me* show Little New Girl
something." So what did Craig show her?—
Craig showed her the beads. "You can string them
in strings," said Craig.

Then Peter said, "Let *me* show Little New Girl
something." So what did Peter show her?—Peter
showed her the clay. "You can make anything
you want out of it," said Peter.

Then Tom said, "Let *me* show Little New Girl
something." So what did Tom show her? Tom
showed her the saw and hammer and nails. "You
can saw or hammer nails," said Tom.

Then Barbara said, "Let me show Little New
Girl something." So what did Barbara show her?
Barbara showed her the paper and scissors. "You
can cut out anything you want," said Barbara.

"Now Little New Girl, what do you want to
do?" said her teacher. And this time the little
girl jumped right up and down and said, "I'm
glad! I want to do everything." "But which thing
first?" asked her teacher. "Let me watch," the
Little New Girl said.

So Little New Girl stood quite still. She saw
Robert go and get some paper and crayons and

sit down at his little table to draw. She saw Virginia get some horses and harness and sit down at her little table to harness them. She saw Craig get some beads and sit down at his little table to string them. She saw Peter get the clay and sit down at his little table to model. She saw Tom go to the bench and begin to saw a piece of wood. She saw Barbara get some paper and scissors and paste and sit down at her little table to cut out and to paste.

Then she said, "I want to draw first." So she took some paper and some colored crayons and she sat down at a little table near the window looking out on the garden. There she drew and she drew and she drew. And she didn't feel like a Little New Girl at all for now she knew where everything was and she knew all the children and she knew her teacher.

THE ROOM WITH THE WINDOW LOOKING
OUT ON THE GARDEN

I know a yellow room
With great big sliding doors
And a window on the side
Looking out upon a garden.
There's a balcony above
With a bench for carpenters
With planes and saws and hammers,
Bang! bang! with nails and hammers.
There are hooks beneath the stairs
To hang up hats and coats,
And nearby there's a sink
With everybody's cup.
There's a rope and there's a slide
Zzzip! but there's a slide.
There are shelves and shelves and shelves
With colored silk and beads,
With paper and with crayons,
And a great big crock with clay.
And the're blocks and blocks and blocks
And blocks and blocks and blocks
And the're horses there and wagons
And cows and dogs and sheep,
And men and women, boys and girls

With clothes upon them too.
And then the're cars to make a train
With engine and caboose.*
And the're lots of little tables
In this yellow, yellow room
For boys and girls to sit at
And play with all those things.
And there's a great big floor
In this yellow, yellow room
For boys and girls to sit on
And play with all those things.
And there is lots of sunshine
In this yellow, yellow room
For boys and girls to sit in
And play with all those things.

* *At this point the teacher might ask, "What else?"*
Not the first time, however. The children must get
the outline as a whole before they contribute. Other-
wise they will be entirely absorbed by the content.

THE MANY-HORSE STABLE

All the material for this story was supplied by a three-year-old. The pattern was added. An older child would not be content with so sketchy an account. But it seems to compass a three-year-old's most significant associations with a stable. The title is one in actual use by a four-year-old class.

THE MANY-HORSE STABLE

Once there was a stable. The stable was in a big city. Downstairs in the stable there were many g-r-e-a-t b-i-g wagons and one little-bit-of-a wagon. And on the walls there were many

g-r-e-a-t b-i-g harnesses and one little-bit-of-a harness. And there were many g-r-e-a-t b-i-g blankets and one little-bit-of-a blanket. And there were some g-r-e-a-t b-i-g whips and one little-bit-of-a whip. And there were some g-r-e-a-t b-i-g nose bags and one little-bit-of-a nose bag. Upstairs in the stalls there were some g-r-e-a-t b-i-g horses and one little-bit-of-a pony.

In the morning the men would come and harness up the g-r-e-a-t b-i-g horses with the g-r-e-a-t b-i-g harnesses to the g-r-e-a-t b-i-g wagons. They would put in the g-r-e-a-t b-i-g blankets and the g-r-e-a-t b-i-g whips and the g-r-e-a-t b-i-g nose bags. Then they would get up on the seats and gather up the reins and off down the street would go the g-r-e-a-t b-i-g horses. Clumpety-lumpety bump! thump! Clumpety-lumpety bump! thump!

Then a little-bit-of-a man would harness up the little-bit-of-a pony with the little-bit-of-a harness to the little-bit-of-a wagon. He would put in the little-bit-of-a blanket and the little-bit-of-a whip and the little-bit-of-a nose bag. Then he would get up on the seat and gather up the reins and off down the street would go the little-bit-of-a pony! Lippety-lippety! lip! lip! lip! Lippety-lippety! lip! lip! lip!

MY KITTY

Here there is no plot. Instead I have attempted to enumerate the associations which cluster
around a kitten and present them in a patterned form.

MY KITTY

Meow, meow!
  Kitty's eyes, two eyes, yellow eyes, shiny bright
    eyes.
Meow, meow!
  Kitty's pointed ears, pink on the inside, fur on
    the outside.
Meow, meow!
  Kitty's mouth, little white teeth and whiskers
    long.
Meow, meow!
  Kitty's fur, soft to stroke like this, like this.

Prrrr, prrrr,
  Little fur ball cuddled close to the warm, warm
    fire.
Prrrr, prrrr,
  Little padded feet pattering soft to get her milk.
Prrrr, prrrr,
  Little pink tongue, lapping up the milk from
    her own little dish.
Prrrr, prrrr,
  Warm little, round little, happy little kitten
    snuggled in my arms.

Pssst, pssst!
  Stiff little kitten, spitting at a dog.
Pssst, pssst!
  Hair standing up on her humped-up back.
Pssst, pssst!
  Sharp white teeth, sharp, sharp, claws.
Pssst, pssst!
  Ready to jump and to bite and to scratch.

  Kitty, kitty, kitty,
    You funny little cat,
  I never know whether you'll purr or spit
    You funny little cat!

THE ROOSTER AND THE HENS
An objective story tied in with the personal.

THE ROOSTER AND THE HENS

Once there was an egg. Inside the egg there was a little chicken growing, for the mother hen had sat on it for three weeks. When the chicken was big enough he wanted to come out and so he went pick, peck, pick, peck, until he made a little hole in the shell. Then he stuck his bill through the hole and wiggled it until the shell cracked and he could get his head through. Then he wiggled it a little more and the shell broke and he could get his foot out. And then the shell broke right in two.

As soon as the little chicken was out he went scritch, scratch, with his little foot. Then he ran to a little saucer of water. He took a little water in his bill; then he held his head up in the air while the water ran down his throat. The mother hen went:

"Cluck, cluck, cluck, cluck, cluck,"

and the little chicken ran to her calling:

"Cheep, cheep, cheep."

Then he heard a funny little noise. He looked around and what do you think he saw? Another egg was cracking because another little chicken was going pick, peck inside. Soon out of the shell came a little baby brother. And then he heard another funny little noise, and another shell broke and out of the shell came a little baby sister. And then he heard another little noise and another shell broke and out of the shell came still another little sister. This went on until there were a lot of yellow baby chickens. Then all the little chickens went scritch, scratch, with their little feet looking for worms, and all the little chickens took a drink of water and held up their heads to let the water run down their throats. And all the little chickens ran to the mother hen calling:

"Cheep, cheep, cheep."

Now all the little chickens began to grow. The little sisters all got little bits of combs on the tops of their heads and under their bills. Their little yellow feathers turned into all kinds of colors. But the little brother chicken, he got a great big red comb on the top of his head and under his bill, and he got long spurs on his ankles. On his neck the feathers grew long and yellow and behind on his tail they grew very long and all shiny green.

He was walking around one morning while it was still dark when suddenly he felt a funny feeling in his throat. He wanted to open his mouth. So he did, and out of his mouth this is what came:

"Cock-a-doodle-doo,
Cock-a-doodle-doo."

He thought it sounded perfectly wonderful; so he opened his mouth again and out came the same sound:

"Cock-a-doodle-doo,
Cock-a-doodle-doo."

Now when his sister hens heard this wonderful rooster-noise they all came running out of the chicken house. This made the rooster more pleased than ever. So he threw his head way back and he opened his beak wide and he crowed:

"Cock-a-doodle-doo,
Cock-a-doodle-doo,
I'm twice as smart as you,
Cock-a-doodle-doo,
See what I can do."

When his sister hens heard him say this each one began to cluck and say:

"Cut-cut-cut, cadaakut,
I'm going to lay an egg, an egg."

Then the rooster answered:

"Cock-a-doodle-do,
I don't believe it's true.
Cock-a-doodle-do,
I don't believe it's true."

So the little black and white hen, she ran into
the barn and up on the side of the wall she saw a
little box. She jumped into the little box and
there she laid an egg. Then she said:

"Cut-cut-cut, cadaakut,
I laid an egg for Robert.
Cut-cut-cut, cadaakut,
I laid an egg for Robert."

Then the little yellow hen she jumped right into
the manger and she wiggled around in the straw
until she made a little nest where she laid an egg.
Then she said:

"Cut-cut-cut, cadaakut,
I laid an egg for Martha.
Cut-cut-cut, cadaakut,
I laid an egg for Martha."

Then the little black hen she saw another little
box nailed on to the wall so she jumped up on
it and she laid an egg and then she said:

> "Cut-cut-cut, cadaakut,
> I laid an egg for Tom, for Tom,
> Cut-cut-cut, cadaakut,
> I laid an egg for Tom."

And then the little white hen she could not find any place at all. She ran around and around. Finally she sat right down in the soft dust which by this time the sun had made all warm, until she made a little round hollow and there she laid an egg. Then she said:

> "Cut-cut-cut, cadaakut,
> I laid an egg for Peter.
> Cut-cut-cut, cadaakut,
> I laid an egg for Peter."

When the rooster saw all these eggs he opened his mouth again and bragged:

> "Cock-a-doodle-doo,
> What they say is true.
> See what they can do,
> Cock-a-doodle-doo."

And the little hens answered:

> "Cut-cut-cut, cadaakut,
> We can lay an egg, an egg,
> Cut-cut-cut, cadaakut,
> We can lay an egg."

And if ever you are out in the country early in the morning you will hear the wonderful rooster-noise. And then you will hear the hens telling how many eggs they have laid for you.

THE LITTLE HEN AND THE ROOSTER

The little hen goes "cut cut cut."
The rooster he goes "cock a doodle doo!
You want me and I want you,
But I'm up here and you're down there."
The little hen goes "cut cut cut,"
The rooster he steps with a funny little strut,
He cocks his eye, gives a funny little sound,
He looks at the hen, he looks all around,
He flaps his wings, he beats the air,
He stretches his neck, then flies to the ground.
"Cock a doodle, cock a doodle, cock a doodle doo!
Now you have me and I have you!"

MY HORSE, OLD DAN

This verse utilizes a child's love of enumeration and of movement. The School has found it the most successful of my verse for small children.

MY HORSE, OLD DAN

Old Dan has two ears
Old Dan has two eyes
Old Dan has one mouth
  With many, many, many, many teeth.

Old Dan has four feet
Old Dan has four hoofs
Old Dan has one tail
  With many, many, many, many hairs.

Old Dan can   w a l k ,   w a l k ,
Old Dan can   trot,   trot,   trot,
Old Dan can run, run, run, run, run, run, run, run,
  Many, many, many, many miles.

Horsie goes jog-a-jog-a-jog
  The wheels go round and round and round.
Horsie goes jog-a-jog-a-jog
  Oh, hear what a rattlety, tattlety sound!
Horsie goes jog-a-jog-a-jog
  The wheels they pound and pound and pound.
Horsie goes jog-a-jog-a-jog
  While the wagon it rattles along the ground!

Auto, auto,
May I have a ride?
Yes, sir, yes, sir,
Step right inside.
Pour in the water,

Turn on the gasolene,
And chug, chug, away we go
Through the country green.

HOW SPOT FOUND A HOME

This story was worked out with the help of a five-year-old boy who supplied most of the content. It at once suggested dramatization to various groups of children to whom it was read. The refrains are definite corner posts in the story and are recognized as such by the children.

HOW SPOT FOUND A HOME

Once there was a cat. She was a black and white and yellow cat and the boys on the street called her Spot. For she was a poor cat with no home but the street. When she wanted to sleep,

she had to hunt for a dark empty cellar. When she wanted to eat, she had to hunt for a garbage can. So poor Spot was very thin and very unhappy. And much of the time she prowled and yowled and howled.

Now one day Spot was prowling along the fence
in the alley. She wanted to find a home. She
was saying to herself:

> "Meow, meow!
> I've no place to eat,
> I've no place to sleep,
> I've only the street!
> Meow, meow, meow!"

Then suddenly she smelled something. Sniff!
went her pink little nose. Spot knew it was smoke
she smelled. The smoke came out of the chimney
of a house. "Where there is smoke there is fire,"
thought Spot, "and where there is fire, it is warm
to lie." So she jumped down from the fence and
on her little padded feet ran softly to the door.
There she saw an empty milk bottle. "Where
there are milk bottles, there is milk," thought Spot,
"and where there is milk, it is good to drink." So
she slipped in through the door.

Inside was a warm, warm kitchen. Spot trotted
softly to the front of the stove and there she curled
up. She was very happy, so she closed her eyes
and began to sing:

> "Purrrr, purrrr,
> Curling up warm
> To a ball of fur,
> I close my eyes

> And purr and purr.
> Purrrr, purrrr,
> Purrrr, purrrr."

Bang! went the kitchen door. Spot opened one sleepy eye. In front of her stood a cross, cross woman. The cross, cross woman scowled. She picked up poor Spot and threw her out of the door, screaming:

> "Scat, scat!
> You old street cat!
> Scat, scat!
> And never come back!"

With a bound Spot jumped back to the fence.

> "Meow, meow!
> I've no place to eat,
> I've no place to sleep,
> I've only the street.
> Meow, meow, meow!"

So she trotted along the fence. In a little while sniff! went her little pink nose again. She smelled more smoke. She stopped by a house with two chimneys. The smoke came out of both chimneys! "Where there are two fires there must be room for me," thought Spot. She jumped off the fence and pattered to the door. By the door there were two empty milk bottles. "Where there is so

much milk there will be some for me," thought
Spot. But the door was shut tight. Spot ran to
the window. It was open! In skipped Spot.
There was another warm, warm kitchen and there
was another stove. Spot trotted softly to the stove
and curled up happy and warm. She closed her
eyes and softly sang:

> "Purrrr, purrrr,
> Curling up warm
> To a ball of fur,
> I close my eyes
> And purr and purr.
> Purrrr, purrrr,
> Purrrr, purrrr."

"Ssssspt!" hissed something close by. Spot leapt
to her feet. "Ssssspt!" she answered back. For
there in front of her stood an enormous black cat.
His back was humped, his hair stood on end, his
eyes gleamed and his teeth showed white.

> "Sssssspt! leave my rug!
> Sssssspt! leave my fire!
> Sssssspt! leave my milk!
> Sssssspt! leave my home!"

Spot gave one great jump out of the window
and another great jump to the top of the fence.
For Spot was little and thin and the great black

cat was strong and big.   And he didn't want Spot
in his home.

Poor Spot trotted along the fence, thinking:

> "Meow, meow,
> I've no place to eat,
> I've no place to sleep,
> I've only the street,
> Meow, meow, meow."

In a little while she smelled smoke again.
Sniff! went her little pink nose.   This time she
stopped by a house with three chimneys.   The
smoke came out of all the chimneys!   "Where
there are three fires there *must* be room for me,"
thought Spot.   So she jumped off the fence and
pattered to the door.   By the door were three
empty milk bottles!   "Where there is so much milk
there must be children," thought Spot and then
she began to feel happy.   But the door was shut
tight.   She trotted to the window.   The window
was shut tight too!   Then she saw some stairs.
Up the stairs she trotted.   There she found another
door and in she slipped.   She heard a very pleasant
sound.

> "I crickle, I crackle,
> I flicker, I flare,
> I jump from nothing right into the air."

There on the hearth burned an open fire with a warm, warm rug in front of it. On the rug was a little table and on the table were two little mugs of milk. Spot curled up on the rug under the table and began to sing:

"Purrrr, purrrr,
Curling up warm
To a ball of fur,
I close my eyes,
And purr and purr.
Purrrr, purrrr,
Purrrr, purrrr."

Pat, pat, pat, pat, pat, pat, pat, pat! Spot heard some little feet coming. A little boy in a night-gown ran into the room. "Look," he called, "at the pretty spotted cat under our table!" Then pat, pat, pat, pat, pat! And a little girl in a night-gown ran into the room. "See," she called, "the pussy has come to take supper with us!" Then the little boy, quick as a wink, put a saucer on the floor and poured some of his milk into it and the little girl, quick as a wink, poured some of hers in too.

In and out, in and out, in and out, went Spot's pink tongue lapping up the milk. Then she sat up and washed her face very carefully. Then she

curled up and closed her eyes and began to sing.
That was her way of saying "Thank you, little
boy and little girl! I'm so glad I've found a
home!"

> "Purrrr, purrrr,
> Purrrr, purrrr,
> Purrrr, purrrr, purrrr."

THE DINNER HORSES
THE GROCERY MAN

The material for these stories came from questions
and observations on the part of three- and four-year-
olds arising largely from their trips on the city streets.
The children should be allowed to name the various
kinds of food.

THE DINNER HORSES

In a certain house on a certain street there lives a certain little girl and her name is Ruth (one of children's names). She sleeps in a little bed in a room with a big window opening on to the street. She sleeps all night in the little bed with her eyes closed tight. In the morning she opens her eyes and it's just beginning to get light. Then she stretches and stretches her legs. Then she stops still and listens. For she hears him coming, coming, coming down the street. Clopperty, clopperty, clopperty, clop! comes the milk horse down the street! He stops in front of Ruth's house. Ruth hears him. Then she hears the driver jump out and pat, pat, pat, she hears his feet coming to the door. Clank, clink, clank, go the milk bottles in his hands. Clank! she hears him put them down. Then fast she hears his feet, pat, pat, pat, pat, pat, pat, pat. "Go on, Dan!" she hears him call, and clopperty, clopperty, clopperty, clop! off goes the milk horse down the street.

Then after a while she hears something else. It's quite light now. Ruth thinks it must be time to get up. She stretches and stretches her legs. Then she stretches and stretches her arms. Then she stops still and listens.

For she hears him coming, coming, coming down the street. Clippety, lip, lip, lip, clippety, lip, lip, lip! comes the bread horse down the street. He stops in front of Ruth's house. Ruth hears him. Then she hears the driver jump out and pat, pat, pat, she hears his feet coming to the door. Rattle, crackle, goes the paper as he puts down the loaves of bread all wrapped up to keep them clean. Then fast she hears his feet, pat, pat, pat, pat, pat, pat, pat. "Go on, Bill!" she hears him call and clippety, lip, lip, lip, clippety, lip, lip, lip! off goes the bread horse down the street.

After breakfast when Ruth is all ready to go to school she hears a big auto coming down the street. Kachug-a-chug-a-chug comes the grocery auto down the street. It stops at Ruth's house. Ruth runs and looks out of the window. She sees the driver jump out and take from the back of the auto a basket all full of things. She can see spinach and potatoes and a package of sugar and——and ——and——.

Then pat, pat, pat, the driver runs to the door. Prrrrrr! she hears the bell ring and Ruth knows that the driver is giving Bessie all the things at the kitchen door. Then pat, pat, pat back comes the driver, jumps into the auto and kachug-a-chug-a-chug! off goes the grocery auto down the street!

On the way to school Ruth passes another wagon. Rattling and clattering, she hears the butcher's wagon come down the street. "Is there anything in that wagon for us?" asks Ruth. And her mother answers, "Yes, a little chicken." Then rattling and clattering off to Ruth's house goes the butcher's wagon down the street.

Now while Ruth is away at school Bessie washes the spinach and chops it up fine and puts it on the stove to boil. She puts the little chicken in a pan and puts it in the oven to roast. Then she puts some big potatoes in the oven to bake. Then she slices some bread and cuts off a piece of butter and pours out some glasses of milk.

When Ruth comes home from school she smells something good. "Dinner's all ready," calls Bessie. Ruth answers, "Come father, come mother. I'm hungry."

So Ruth and her father and mother sit down at the table and they drink the milk and they eat the bread and the spinach and the potatoes and the chicken which the milk horse and the bread horse and the grocery auto and the butcher's wagon brought in the morning.

THE GROCERY MAN

Prrrip! prrrip! prrrip! the telephone rings in the grocery store. "Hello," says the grocery man. "Who are you?"

"I'm Ruth's mother. Good morning, Mr. Grocery Man."

"Good morning, Ruth's Mother. What can I send you today?"

"Please, Mr. Grocery Man, send me some potatoes and some graham crackers and a package of sugar and some carrots."

"Is that all, Ruth's Mother?"

"Yes, that's all. Goodbye, Mr. Grocery Man."

"Goodbye, Ruth's Mother."

So the grocery man hangs up the telephone and takes a basket and in the basket he puts some potatoes, some graham crackers, a package of sugar and some carrots.

Then prrrip! prrrip! prrrip! the telephone rings again.

"Hello!" says the Grocery Man. "Who is this?"

"This is John's Mother. Good morning, Mr. Grocery Man."

"Good morning, John's Mother. What can I send you today?"

"Please, Mr. Grocery Man, send me some spinach and some apples and some butter and some eggs."

"Is that all, John's Mother?"

"Yes, that's all. Goodbye, Mr. Grocery Man."

"Goodbye, John's Mother."

So the Grocery Man hangs up the telephone and takes another basket and in the basket he puts some spinach and some apples and some butter and some eggs.

Then prrrip! prrrip, prrrip! the telephone rings another time.

"Hello!" says the Grocery Man. "Who are you?"

"I'm Robert's Mother. Good morning, Mr. Grocery Man."

"Good morning, Robert's Mother. What can I send you today?"

"Please, Mr. Grocery Man, send me some prunes and some macaroni and some salt and some oatmeal."

"Is that all, Robert's Mother?"

"Yes, that's all. Goodbye, Mr. Grocery Man."

"Goodbye, Robert's Mother."

So the Grocery Man hangs up the telephone
and takes another basket and in the basket he
puts some prunes and some macaroni and some
salt and some oatmeal. Then he carries Ruth's
basket out and puts it in a wagon on the street.
Then he carries John's basket out and puts it in
the wagon. At last he carries Robert's basket out
and puts that in the wagon with the others. Then
the driver jumps to the seat and gathers up the
reins and says "Go on, Old Dan," and clopperty,
clopperty clop! off goes Old Dan down the street.

Old Dan goes clopperty, clopperty, clop till he
gets to Ruth's house and there he stops. The driver
jumps out and takes the basket and pat, pat, pat,
go his feet running to the door. Prrrr! he rings
the bell and gives Ruth's mother the potatoes, the
graham crackers, the sugar and the carrots. Then
pat, pat, pat, he is back in the wagon. "Go on,
Old Dan," and clopperty, clopperty, clop! off goes
Old Dan down the street.

Old Dan goes clopperty, clopperty, clop till he
gets to John's house and there he stops. The driver
jumps out and takes another basket and pat, pat,
pat go his feet running to the door. Prrrr! he
rings the bell and gives John's mother the spinach,
the apples, the butter and the eggs. Then pat, pat,

pat, he is back in the wagon. "Go on, Old Dan," and clopperty, clopperty, clop! off goes Old Dan down the street.

Old Dan goes clopperty, clopperty, clop till he gets to Robert's house and there he stops. The driver jumps out, takes another basket and pat, pat, pat, he is at the door. Prrrr! he rings the bell and gives Robert's mother the prunes, the macaroni, the salt and the oatmeal. Then pat, pat, pat, he is back in the wagon. "Go on, Old Dan," and clopperty, clopperty, clop! off goes old Dan down the street.

So Old Dan goes clopperty, clopperty, clop from house to house until he has left a basket with everybody who telephoned to the grocery man in the morning.

THE JOURNEY

This story, which is an adaptation of a five-year-old's story quoted in the introduction, embodies the details given to me by another three-year-old child. The sound of the train should be intoned, as it was in the original telling.

THE JOURNEY

Once Ruth's father was going to take a journey. He got out his suitcase. And in his suitcase he put his slippers, his pajamas, his tooth brush, some tooth paste, some clean underclothes, some clean shirts, some collars, some socks and some handkerchiefs. Then he kissed Ruth goodbye as she lay asleep in her bed and he kissed her mother goodbye and with his suitcase in his hand went up to the Pennsylvania Station.

At the train he met the negro porter. "What berth, sir?" said the porter. "Lower 10", said Ruth's father. So the porter took the suitcase and put it down at Number 10 which was all made up into two beds, one above the other, with green curtains hanging in front. Then Ruth's father undressed. And in a few minutes he was asleep behind the green curtains.

Soon the train started and Ruth's father never woke up. "Thum," said the train (on many different keys) all through the night. "Thum, thum, thum; thum, thum, thum, thum; thum, thum, thum, thum; thum, thum, thum, thum. *Philadel-*

phial Thum, thum, thum, thum; thum, thum, thum, thum; thum, thum, thum, thum; thum, thum, thum, thum. *Baltimore!* Thum, thum, thum, thum; thum, thum, thum, thum; thum, thum, thum; thum, thum, thum, thum. *Washington!*

Then Ruth's father got up and dressed himself, for it was morning. The negro porter carried his suitcase to the platform. "Goodbye, sir," he said. "Goodbye, Porter," said Ruth's father. And then he went off to a hotel.

The next day it was time for him to go home. So Ruth's father packed his suitcase again. In his suitcase he put his slippers, his pajamas, his tooth brush, some tooth paste, his dirty underclothes, his dirty shirts, his collars, his socks and his handkerchiefs. Then he went to the Pennsylvania Station in Washington.

At the train he met another negro porter. "What berth, sir?" said the porter. "Upper 6," said Ruth's father. So the porter took the suitcase and put it in the top bed of Number 6. Ruth's father climbed up into the upper berth. Then he undressed and in a few minutes he was asleep behind the green curtains.

Soon the train started. "Thum," said the train, though Ruth's father never heard it he was so sound asleep. "Thum, thum, thum, thum; thum, thum, thum, thum; thum, thum, thum, thum; thum, thum, thum, thum. *Baltimore!* Thum, thum, thum, thum; thum, thum, thum, thum; thum, thum, thum, thum; thum, thum, thum, thum. *Philadelphia!* Thum, thum, thum, thum; thum, thum, thum, thum; thum, thum, thum, thum; thum, thum, thum, thum. *New York!*"

Then Ruth's father got up and dressed himself for it was morning. The negro porter carried his suitcase to the platform. "Goodbye, sir," he said. "Goodbye, Porter," said Ruth's father.

Then Ruth's father jumped into a taxi and in a few minutes he was at home. Ruth came running down the stairs. "Here's father," she cried. "Here's father in time for breakfast!" "My," said Ruth's father, giving her a hug, "It's good to be home!"

PEDRO'S FEET

Here there is a definite attempt to let the sounds tell their own story.

PEDRO'S FEET

Little Pedro was a dog. He lived in New York City. He was owned by a little boy who loved him. For Pedro had big brown eyes and curly brown hair and when he wanted anything he would go:

"Hu-u-u, hu-u-u, hu-u-u!" And any one would have loved Pedro.

One day Pedro was lying on his front steps in the warm, warm sun. He put his nose on his little fore paws and went to sleep.

"Bzbzbzbzbzbzbzbzbz!" went a little fly in his ear.

"Yap, yap!" went Pedro's jaws as he snapped at the fly. But he missed the fly.

"Bzbzbzbzbzbzbzbzbz!" went the little fly.

"Yap, yap!" went Pedro's jaws. But he missed the fly again.

"Bzbzbzbzbzbzbzbzbz!"

"Yap, yap, yap!"

"Bzbzbzbzbzbzbzbzbz!"

"Yap, yap, yap, yap!"

Up jumped Pedro. "I can't sleep with that fly

149

in my ear! I'll take a walk!" Down the steps
he went. Skippety, skippety, skippety, skippety.
He reached the sidewalk. On the sidewalk went
his feet. You could hear them as they beat. Pitter patter, pitter patter, pitter patter down the
street.

When he came to the end of the block, he started
across the street. Pitter patter, pitter patter, pitter pat——

"Honk, honk! Look out, look out! Honk,
honk!"

Jump-thump! went Pedro's feet. Jump-jump
jump-jump, jump-jump, thump-thump, thump-
thump, thump-thump, jump-jump, jump-jump,
jump-jump, pitter patter, pitter patter,—he'd
reached the other side! And the auto hadn't hurt
him!

Again on the sidewalk went his feet. You could
hear them as they beat pitter patter, pitter patter,
pitter patter down the street.

When he came to the end of this block, he
started across the next street.

Pitter patter, pitter patter, pitter pat——

"Clopperty, clopperty, clopperty, clopperty!
Get out of my way, get out of my way! Clopperty, clopperty, clopperty, clopperty!"

Jump-thump! went Pedro's feet. Jump-jump
jump-jump, jump-jump, thump-thump, thump-
thump, thump-thump, jump-jump, jump-jump,
jump-jump, pitter patter, pitter patter,—he'd
reached the other side! And the horse hadn't hurt
him either!

Again on the sidewalk went his feet. You could
hear them as they beat,—pitter patter, pitter patter,
pitter patter down the street.

When he came to the end of this block, he
started across the next street.

Pitter patter, pitter patter, pitter pat—— Pedro
stopped with one little front foot up in the air.
In the middle of the street stood a man. He had
on high rubber boots and he held a big hose.

Shrzshrzshrzshrzshrz—came the water out of
the hose. It hit the street. Splsh splsh splsh splsh
splsh! It ran in a little stream into the hole in
the gutter,—gubble, gubble, gubble, gubble, gubble! This was something new to Pedro. He didn't
understand.

Pitter patter, pitter patter, pitter patter. He
thought he'd better find out about it.

"Hie, you little dog! Look out!" shouted the
man.

Pitter patter, pitter patter, pitter patter.

"Hie, you little dog. I say look out!"

Pitter patter, pitter pat—ssssssssss bang! the water hit him!

"Ki-eye! yow! yow!" Kathump, kathump, kathump, kathump; kathump, kathump, kathump, kathump! Fast, fast went Pedro's feet, running, tearing down the street.

"Ki-eye! I'm going home!" Kathump, kathump, kathump, kathump! Down the sidewalk, 'cross the street, 'nother sidewalk, 'nother street, kathump, kathump, kathump, kathump! Pedro was at home. Skippety, skippety up the stairs. Pedro was at his own front door.

He stopped. Brrrrrrrrrrrrr—he shook himself. He scattered the water all around.

"Bow, wow, I'm glad I'm home! Bow, wow, I'm glad I'm home!"

Then he lay down in the warm, warm sun. And he put his nose on his little fore paws. And he closed his eyes and he went to sleep.

"Bzbzbzbzbzbzbzbzbz!"

But Pedro was too sound asleep to hear the fly.

"Whe-whuhuhu, whe-whuhuhu, whe-whuhuhu." That's the way he was breathing. For he was oh, so sound asleep! And there he is sleeping now.

HOW THE ENGINE LEARNED
THE KNOWING SONG

This story stresses the relationship of use in response to what seems to be a five-year-old method of thinking.

The school has found it best to let the younger children take the parts individually but to omit the parts in unison. The joy of the mere noise makes it difficult to bring them back for the close of the story. All the children have repeated the refrains after a few readings with evident enjoyment.

HOW THE ENGINE LEARNED THE
KNOWING SONG

Once there was a new engine. He had a great
big boiler; he had a smoke stack; he had a bell;
he had a whistle; he had a sand-dome; he had
a headlight; he had four big driving wheels; he
had a cab. But he was very sad, was this engine,
for he didn't know how to use any of his parts.
All around him on the tracks were other engines,
puffing or whistling or ringing their bells and
squirting steam. One big engine moved his wheels
slowly, softly muttering to himself, "I'm going,
I'm going, I'm going." Now the new engine knew
this was the end of the Knowing Song of Engines.
He wanted desperately to sing it. So he called
out:

> "I want to go
> But I don't know how;
> I want to know,
> Please teach me now.
> Please somebody teach me how."

Now there were two men who had come just
on purpose to teach him how. And who do you

suppose they were? The engineer and the fireman! When the engineer heard the new engine
call out, he asked, "What do you want, new
engine?"

And the engine answered:

> "I want the sound
> Of my wheels going round.
> I want to stream
> A jet of steam.
> I want to puff
> Smoke and stuff.
> I want to ring
> Ding, ding-a-ding.
> I want to blow
> My whistle so.
> I want my light
> To shine out bright.
> I want to go ringing and singing the song,
> The humming song of the engine coming,
> The clear, near song of the engine here,
> The knowing song of the engine going."

Now the engineer and the fireman were pleased
when they heard what the new engine wanted.
But the engineer said:

> "All in good time, my engine,
> Steady, steady,
> 'Til you're ready.
> Learn to know
> Before you go."

Then he said to the fireman, "First we must give our engine some water." So they put the end of a hose hanging from a big high-up tank right into

a little tank under the engine's tender. The water filled up this little tank and then ran into the big boiler and filled that all up too. And while they were doing this the water kept saying:

"I am water from a stream
When I'm hot I turn to steam."

When the engine felt his boiler full of water he asked eagerly:

"Now I have water,
Now do I know
How I should go?"

But the fireman said:

"All in good time, my engine,
Steady, steady,
'Til you're ready,
Learn to know
Before you go."

Then he said to the engineer, "Now we must give
our engine some coal." So they filled the tender
with coal, and then under the boiler the fireman
built a fire. Then the fireman began blowing and
the coals began glowing. And as he built the
fire, the fire said:

"I am fire,
The coal I eat
To make the heat
To turn the stream
Into the steam."

When the engine felt the sleeping fire wake up
and begin to live inside him and turn the water
into steam he said eagerly:

"Now I have water,
Now I have coal,
Now do I know
How I should go?"

But the engineer said:

> "All in good time, my engine,
> Steady, steady,
> 'Til you're ready.
> Learn to know
> Before you go."

Then he said to the fireman, "We must oil our engine well." So they took oil cans with funny long noses and they oiled all the machinery, the piston-rods, the levers, the wheels, everything that moved or went round. And all the time the oil kept saying:

> "No creak,
> No squeak."

When the engine felt the oil smoothing all his machinery, he said eagerly:

> "Now I have water,
> Now I have coal,
> Now I am oiled,
> Now do I know
> How I should go?"

But the fireman said:

> "All in good time, my engine,
> Steady, steady,
> 'Til you're ready.
> Learn to know
> Before you go."

Then he said to the engineer, "We must give our engine some sand." So they took some sand and they filled the sand domes on top of the boiler so that he could send sand down through his two little pipes and sprinkle it in front of his wheels when the rails were slippery. And all the time the sand kept saying:

> "When ice drips,
> And wheel slips,
> I am sand
> Close at hand."

When the new engine felt his sand-dome filled with sand he said eagerly:

> "Now I have water,
> Now I have coal,
> Now I am oiled,
> Now I have sand,
> Now do I know
> How I should go?"

But the engineer said:

> "All in good time, my engine,
> Steady, steady,
> 'Til you're ready.
> Learn to know
> Before you go."

Then he said to the fireman, "We must light our engine's headlight." So the fireman took a cloth

and he wiped the mirror behind the light and
polished the brass around it. Then he filled the
lamp with oil. Then the engineer struck a match
and lighted the lamp and closed the little door
in front of it. And all the time the light kept
saying:

> "I'm the headlight shining bright
> Like a sunbeam through the night."

Now when the engine saw the great golden path
of brightness streaming out ahead of him, he said
eagerly:

> "Now I have water,
> Now I have coal,
> Now I am oiled,
> Now I have sand,
> Now I make light,
> Now do I know
> How I should go?"

And the engineer said, "We will see if you are
ready, my new engine." So he climbed into the
cab and the fireman got in behind him. Then he
said, "Engine, can you blow your whistle so?"
And he pulled a handle which let the steam into
the whistle and the engine whistled (who wants
to be the whistle?) "Toot, toot, toot." Then he
said, "Can you puff smoke and stuff?" And the
engine puffed black smoke (who wants to be the

smoke?), saying, "Puff, puff, puff, puff, puff."
Then he said, "Engine, can you squirt a stream of
steam?" And he opened a valve (who wants to
be the steam?) and the engine went, "Szszszszsz."
Then he said, "Engine, can you sprinkle sand?"
And he pulled a little handle (who wants to be
the sand?) and the sand trickled drip, drip, drip,
down on the tracks in front of the engine's wheels.
Then he said, "Engine, does your light shine out
bright?" And he looked (who wants to be the
headlight?) and there was a great golden flood
of light on the track in front of him. Then he
said, "Engine, can you make the sound of your
wheels going round?" And he pulled another
lever and the great wheels began to move (who
wants to be the wheels?) Then the engineer said:

> "Now is the time,
> Now is the time.
> Steady, steady,
> Now you are ready.

Blow whistle, ring bell, puff smoke, hiss steam, sprinkle
sand, shine light, turn wheels!

> 'Tis time to be ringing and singing the song,
> The humming song of the engine coming,
> The clear, near song of the engine here,
> The knowing song of the engine going."

Then whistle blew, bell rang, smoke puffed, steam hissed, sand sprinkled, light shone and wheels turned like this: (Eventually the children can do this together, each performing his chosen part.)

"Toot-toot, ding-a-ding, puff-puff,
Szszszszsz, drip-drip, chug-chug."

(After a moment stop the children)
That's the way the new engine sounded when he started on his first ride and didn't know how to do things very well. But that's not the way he sounded when he had learned to go really smooth and fast. Then it was that he learned *really* to sing "The Knowing Song of the Engine." He sang it better than any one else for he became the fastest, the steadiest, the most knowing of all express engines. And this is the song he sang. You could hear it humming on the rails long before he came and hear it humming on the rails long after he had passed. Now listen to the song.

(Begin very softly rising to a climax with "I'm here" and gradually dying to a faint whisper)

"I'm coming, I'm coming, I'm coming, I'm coming,
I'm coming, I'm coming, I'm coming, I'm coming,
I'm coming, I'm coming, I'm coming, I'm coming.
I'm Coming, I'm Coming, I'm Coming, I'm Coming,

I'M HERE, I'M HERE, I'M HERE, I'M
  HERE,
I'M HERE, I'M HERE, I'M HERE, I'M
  HERE.
I'm Going, I'm Going, I'm Going, I'm Going,
I'm going, I'm going, I'm going, I'm going,
I'm going, I'm going, I'm going, I'm going,
I'm going, I'm going, I'm going, I'm going."

THE FOG BOAT STORY

The refrains must be intoned if not sung to get the proper effect. Most of the informational parts of the original story have been cut out. The story grew out of questions asked before breakfast on foggy days, and was originally told to the sound of the distant fog horns.

THE FOG BOAT STORY

Early, early one morning, all the fog boats were talking. This is the way they were going:

"Toot, toot, toot, too-oot, to-oo-oot!" (on many different keys.)

Way down at the wharf a big steamer was being pulled out into the river. The furnaces were all going for the stokers were down in the hole shoveling coal, down in the hole shoveling coal, shoveling coal, and a lot of black smoke was coming out of the smoke stack. And the engines were working, chug, chug, chug. And all the baggage and freight had been put down in the hold. And all the food had been put on the ice. And all the passengers were on board and the gang-plank had been pulled up. And this is what the big steamer was saying:

"Toot toot I'm mov - ing; toot toot I'm mov - ing."

And do you know what was making the steamer move? What was pulling her out into the river? It was a little tug boat and the tug boat had hold of one end of a big rope and the other end of the rope was tied fast to the steamer. And the little tug boat was puffing and chucking and working away as hard as he could and calling out:

"Too too too too toot I'm aw - ful smart; too too too too toot I pull big things."

And do you know why the tug boat and the steamer were talking like this? It is because they were afraid they might bump into some other ship in the fog for they can't see in the fog. You know how white and thick the fog can be.

So the old steamer and the little tug boat both kept tooting until they were way out in the middle of the river.

"Toot, toot, I'm moving." "Tootootootootoot, I'm awful smart."

Now when they were way out in the middle of the river, the little tug boat dropped the rope from the big steamer and turned around. As it puffed away it called out:

> "Too-too-too-tootoot, I'm going home
> Too-too-too-tootoot, I'm awful smart."

Then the big steamer moved slowly down the river towards the great ocean calling through the fog:

"Toot, toot, I'm moving."

Up on the captain's bridge stood the pilot. He is the man who tells just where to make the steamer go in the harbor. He knows where everything is. He knows where the rocks are on the right and he didn't let the steamer bump them. He knows where the sand reef is on the left and he didn't let the steamer get on to that. He knows just where the deep water is and he kept the steamer in it all the time.

Now down on the right so close that it almost bumped, there went a flat boat. This boat was saying:

"Toot toot My load is heavy,   load is heavy, load is heavy,   toot,"

And that was a coal barge. And then down on the left so close that it almost bumped on the other side they heard another boat saying:

"Too toot, back & forth; Too toot, back & forth"

And that was a ferry boat! Then off on the right they heard a great big deep voice. This is what it said:

"Toot   toot,   'tis   I"

And that was a war boat! And every time the old
steamer answered:

"Toot, toot, I'm moving."

Once off on the left the passengers could hear
this:

"Ding——g! dong——g!
Hear my song——g!
Ding——g! dong——g!"

And what bell do you think that was way out
there? A bell buoy rocking on the water! Every
time the wave went up it said, "ding" and every
time the wave went down it said, "dong."

By this time the old steamer was out of the harbor way out in the open sea. The pilot came
down from the captain's deck; he climbed down
the rope ladder to the little pilot boat that was
tied close to the big steamer. Then the little pilot
boat pushed away into the fog calling:

"Too too toot too toot   I'm go - ing go - ing home"

And again the big steamer answered:

"Toot, toot, I'm moving."

Then way off on the left so far away it could barely hear it, it heard:

"Don't hit me, toot toot, don't hit me, toot toot"

And that was a sail boat! Then way off on the right so far away it could barely hear it, it heard

"Toot, toot, I'm moving"

and that was another steamer.

And again the big steamer answered:

"Toot, toot, I'm moving."

And so the old steamer went out into the fog calling, calling so that no boat would hit it. And all the other boats that passed it, they went calling, calling too.

HAMMER AND SAW AND PLANE

This story is a slight extension of the children's own experience. It is purposely limited to the tools they themselves handle familiarly.

HAMMER AND SAW AND PLANE

Once there was a carpenter. He had built himself a fine new house. And now it was all done. The walls, the floors and the roof were done. The stairs were done. The windows and doors were done. And the carpenter had moved into his new house.

In his house he had a stove and he had electric lights. He had beds and chairs and bureaus and bookcases. He had everything except a table to eat off of. He still had to stand up when he ate his meals!

So the carpenter thought he would make him a table. But he had no lumber left. So off he went to the lumber mill. At the lumber mill he saw lots and lots of lumber piled in the yard. The carpenter told the man at the lumber mill just how much lumber he wanted and just how long he wanted it and how broad he wanted it and how thick he wanted it.

So the man at the lumber mill put all this lumber,—just what the carpenter had ordered,—on a wagon and sent it out to the carpenter's house.

And then the carpenter began. He said to himself, "First I must make my boards just the right
length."   So he measured a board just as long as

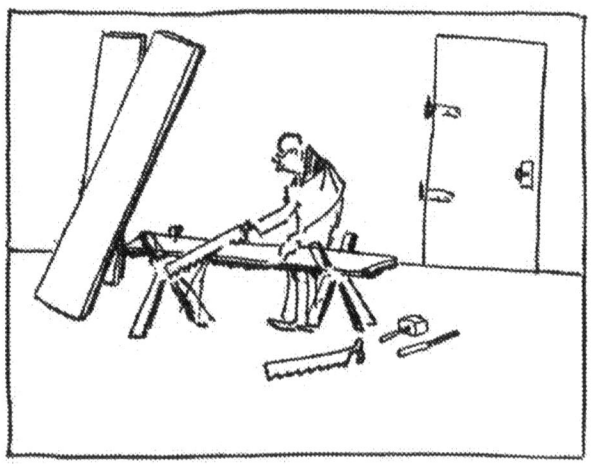

he wanted the top to be; then he put the board
on a sawhorse and he took his saw and began to
saw:

> "Zzzu," went the saw,
> "Zzzu, zzzu, zzzu."
>   The sawdust flew
>   The saw ripped through
> Down dropped the board sawed right in two.

And then the carpenter took another board and
he measured this just the same length.   Then he

put this board on the sawhorse and he took the
saw and began to saw:

> "Zzzu," went the saw,
> "Zzzu, zzzu, zzzu."
> The sawdust flew
> The saw ripped through
> Down dropped the board sawed right in two.

And then the carpenter took still another board
and "Zzzu," went the saw until this board too was
sawed right in two. Then he had enough for the
top of the table. Then he took the pieces that were
going to make the legs and he sawed four of them
just the right length. Then he sawed the boards
that were going to be the braces until they too were
just the right length. And underneath his sawhorse there was a little pile of sawdust.

Then after this the carpenter says to himself, "I
must make my boards smooth." So he puts a board
in the vise and he begins to plane the board.

> The plane he guides
> The plane it glides
> It smooths, it slides
> All over the sides.

And when this board is all smooth, the carpenter
takes it out of the vise and puts in another board.
Then he takes his plane.

> The plane he guides
> The plane it glides
> It smooths, it slides
> All over the sides.

And then the carpenter takes still another board and he guides and slides the plane until this board too is all smooth. And he does this until all the boards that are going to make the top and the legs and the braces are all smooth. And underneath his bench there is a pile of shavings.

And then the carpenter he says to himself, "I must nail my boards together." So he puts the boards that are going to make the top together and he takes a nail and then he swings his hammer:

> The hammer it gives a swinging pound.
> The nail it gives a ringing sound.
>   Bing! bang! bing! bing!
> And the boards are tight together!

And then the carpenter takes another piece of the top and puts it beside the other two and he takes another nail and then he swings his hammer again.

> The hammer it gives a swinging pound.
> The nail it gives a ringing sound.
>   Bing! bang! Bing! bing!
> And the boards are tight together!

And then the carpenter takes one piece that is going to be a leg and he holds it so it stands right out from the top, and he takes another nail and he nails the leg to the top. Bing! bang! bing! bing! He does this with the other three legs of his table. And then he has four strong legs and the top of his table all nailed together.

Then the carpenter he says to himself, "I'll put some boards across and make it stronger." So he takes some boards sawed just the right length, and he nails them across underneath the top, bing! bang! bing! bing! And then he has a table!

So the carpenter lifts his table out into the middle of his room and he puts a chair beside it. When he sits down he is smiling all over. For the table is just the right size and just the right height and it is strong and good to look at. The carpenter is so glad to have a table to eat off of that he says to himself:

> "Now isn't it grand?
> I won't have to stand
> While eating my dinner again!
> For now I am able
> To sit at the table
> I made with saw, hammer and plane!"

THE ELEPHANT

This was written with the help of eight-year-old children who were trying to make everything sound "heavy" and "slow."

THE ELEPHANT

The little boy had never before been to the Zoo.
He walked up close to the high iron fence. On
the other side he saw a huge wrinkled grey lump
slowly sway to one side and then slowly sway back
to the other. And as it swayed from side to side
its great long wrinkled trunk swung slowly too.
The little boy followed the trunk with his eye up
to the huge head of the great wrinkled grey lump.
There were enormous torn worn flapping ears.
And there, too, embedded like jewels in a leather
wall sparkled two little eyes. These eyes were
fastened on the little boy. They seemed to shine
in the dull wrinkled skin. Slowly the huge mass
began to move. Slowly one heavy padded foot
came up and then went down with a soft thud.
Then came another soft thud and another and another. Suddenly the monstrous trunk waved,
curled, lifted, stretched and stretched, until its soft
pink end was thrust through the high iron fence
and the little boy could look up into the fleshy
yawning red mouth. The little boy drew back
from the high iron fence. The end of the trunk

wiggled and wriggled around feeling its way up and down a rod of the fence; the great body swayed from one heavy foot to the other; and all the time the bright little eyes were fastened on the boy.

The little boy looked and looked and looked again. He could hardly believe his eyes. "Whew!" he said at last, "so that's an elephant!"

HOW THE ANIMALS MOVE

The classifications and most of the expressions were suggested by a child.

HOW THE ANIMALS MOVE

The lion, he has paws with claws,
   The horse, he walks on hooves,
The worm, he lies right on the ground
   And wriggles when he moves!

The seal, he moves with swimming feet,
   The moth, has wings like a sail,
The fly he clings; the bird he wings,
   The monkey swings by his tail!

      But boys and girls
      With feet and hands
      Can walk and run
      And swim and stand!

THE SEA-GULL

All the material and most of the expressions are taken from a story by a six-year-old. It was put into rhythm because the children wished "the words to go like the waves."

THE SEA-GULL

Feel the waves go rocking, rocking,
  Feel them roll and roll and roll.
On the top there sits a sea-gull
  And he's rocking with the waves.
Now 'tis evening and he's weary
  So he's resting on the waves.

When he woke in early morning
  Like a flash he spied a fish.
Quick he flew and quickly diving
  Snapped the fish and ate him straight.
Then he screamed for he was happy.
  Then he spied another fish
Quick he flew and quickly diving
  Snapped the fish and ate him straight.
So he played while shone the sunshine,
  Catching fish and screaming hoarse
Till he was quite out of hunger,
  And would rest him on the waves.
Once he flapped and flapped his great wings,
  Soaring like an aeroplane.
Down below him lay the ocean

Like a wrinkled crinkly thing,
And giant steamers looked like toy ones
Slowly moving on the waves.

Now the moonshine's making silver
  All the tossing, rocking waves.
And the sea-gull looks like silver
  And his great wings look like silver
  Pressing close his silver side,
And his sharp beak looks like silver
  Tucked beneath his silver wings.
For beneath the silver moonlight
  See, the sea-gull's gone to sleep.
Rocking, rocking on the water,
Sleeping, sleeping on the waves,
Rocking—sleeping—sleeping—rocking,
Fast asleep upon the waves.

THE FARMER TRIES TO SLEEP

It has seemed appropriate to let the children realize the incessant quality of farm work before that of the factory.

THE FARMER TRIES TO SLEEP

The farmer woke up in the morning
  And sleepy as sleepy was he,
He turned in his bed and he grouchily said:
  "Today I will sleep! Let me be, let me be!
  Today I will sleep! Let me be!"

Now Puss in the corner she heard
  She heard what the farmer had said,
She ran to the barn and she mewed in alarm;
  "The farmer will sleep in his bed, in his bed!
  Today he will sleep in his bed!"

Then Horse in the stable looked up,
  He whinneyed and shook his old head;
"Shall I stand here all day without any hay?
  Whey-ey-ey! Farmer, come feed me!" he said,
    so he said,
  "Whey-ey-ey! Farmer, come feed me!" he said.

But the farmer he tight closed his eyes
  For sleepy as sleepy was he,
He turned in his bed and he angrily said:
  "Horse, I will sleep! Let me be, let me be!
  Horse, I will sleep! Let me be!"

Down under the barn in the dirt
  Pig heard what the Pussy cat mewed.
"Can he give me the scraps when he's taking his
    naps?
  Wee-ee, Farmer, come give me my food, oh, my
    food!
  Wee-ee, Farmer, come give me my food!"

But the farmer he tight closed his ears
  For sleepy as sleepy was he,
He turned in his bed and he sulkily said:
  "Pig, I will sleep! Let me be, let me be!
  Pig, I will sleep! Let me be!"

Now Rooster with Chickens and Hen
  Had been crowing since early that morn,
And he crowed when he heard this terrible word:
  "Cock-a-doo! Farmer, give us our corn, us our
    corn!
  Cock-a-doo! Farmer, give us our corn."

But the farmer he pulled up the covers
  For sleepy as sleepy was he,
He turned in his bed and crossly he said:
  "Cock, I will sleep! Let me be, let me be!
  Cock, I will sleep! Let me be!"

Cow heard in the pasture and lowed;
  "My cud no longer I chew,
I stand by the gate and I wait and I wait,
  Oh, Farmer, come milk me! Moo-oo, moo-oo!
  Oh, Farmer, come milk me, moo-oo!"

But the farmer got under the covers,
  For sleepy as sleepy was he,
He turned in his bed and fiercely he said,
  "Cow, I will sleep! Let me be, let me be!
  Cow, I will sleep! Let me be!"

Then Horse he broke from the stable,
  And Pig he broke from the pen,
And Cow jumped the fence though she hadn't
      much sense,
  And Cock called Chickens and Hen, and Hen,
  He called to Chickens and Hen.

Then up to the farm house door
  All followed the Pussy who knew.
Horse whinneyed, Cock crowed, Pig grunted, Cow
      lowed;
  "Get up, Farmer! Whey, cock-a-doo, wee-wee-
      wee, mooo!
  Whey, cock-a-doo, wee-wee-wee, moooo!"

The farmer down under the covers,
  He heard and he groaned and he sighed.
He wearily rose and he put on his clothes;
  "They need me, I'm coming, I'm coming," he
      cried,
  "They need me, I'm coming," he cried.

"I'll feed Horse, Chickens and Pig,
  I'll milk old Cow," said he,
"And when this is done, my work's just begun,
  Today I must work, so I see, so I see!
  Today I must work, so I see!"

So he fed Horse, Chickens and Pig
  And afterwards milked old Cow.
For Farmer must work, he never can shirk!
  Today he is working, right now, right now!
  Today he is working right now!

WONDERFUL-COW-THAT-NEVER-WAS!

All the essential points in this story were taken from the story of a four-year-old's about a horse. He enjoyed the nonsense in telling it. Some of the four-year-old groups have appreciated the humor; some five-year-olds have not. Instead they have seemed confused.

WONDERFUL-COW-THAT-NEVER-WAS!

Once there was a wonderful cow,—only she never was! She always had been wonderful, ever since she was a baby calf. Her mother noticed it at once. She was born out in the pasture one sunny morning in June. As soon as she was born, she got up on her long, thin legs. She wobbled quite a little for she wasn't very strong. Then she went over to her mother and put her nose down to her mother's bag and took a drink of milk. This is what all the old cow's babies had always done so the old cow thought nothing of that. But when this wonderful last baby calf had drunk its breakfast, what do you suppose it did? It stood on its head! Now the old cow had never seen anything like this. It was most surprising! It frightened her. She called to it:

> "Oh, my baby, baby calf,
> Your mother kindly begs,
> Please, *please* get off your head
> And stand upon your legs!"

But the baby calf only mooed. And it smiled when it mooed which the old cow thought queer too. None of her other babies had smiled. Then the calf said:

> "I'm a wonderful calf,
> And it makes me laugh
> Such wonderful things can I do!
> I stand on my head
> Whenever I'm fed,
> And smile whenever I moo,
> I do,
> I smile whenever I moo!"

"Dear me!" thought the old mother cow. "I never saw or heard anything like this!"

But this was only the beginning. The baby calf kept on doing strange and wonderful things till at last everyone called her Wonderful-calf-that-never-was! And many people used to come to see her stand on her head whenever she was fed. She did other queer things too! Once she pulled off the ear of another calf! And all she said was: "Poor little calf! You mustn't go in the pasture where there are other calves!" But the little calf who had lost its ear said, "Yes, I must!" But after that Wonderful-calf-that-never-was was kept in the barn for a long time.

At last it was June again and she was a year old.

Her horns had begun to grow. The old cow, her mother, had another baby. This new baby calf was just like other calves and not wonderful at all. The old cow was glad for Wonderful-cow-that-never-was worried her very much. For everything about her was queer. One day the calf who had lost the ear,—she was a young cow now, —took hold of the tail of Wonderful-young-cow-that-never-was and pulled it. And what do you suppose happened? The tail broke right off! All the cows were frightened. Whoever heard of a broken tail? But Wonderful-young-cow-that-never-was only mooed and when she mooed she always smiled. Then she said:

> "I'm a wonderful cow
> And I don't know how
> Such wonderful things I do!
> If I break my tail,
> I never fail
> To glue with a grasshopper's goo,
> I do,
> I glue with a grasshopper's goo!"

And so she did. She got a grasshopper to give her some sticky stuff and she smeared it on the two ends of her broken tail and stuck them together. "And now it's as good as new," she said, "and now it's as good as new!"

Her horns grew and grew. She was very proud of them and was always trying to hook some one or gore another cow with them. But one day she went to the edge of the lake when it was very still. It wasn't wavy at all. And as she leaned over to drink, she saw herself in the water. My mercy! but she was shocked!

"My horns are straight!" she screamed, "and I want them curly!" She ran to the old mother cow and had what her mother called the "Krink-kranks." She jumped up and down and bellowed: "My horns are straight and I want them curly!"

The old mother cow was giving her new baby some milk. It made her cross to hear Wonderful-cow-that-never-was having krink-kranks over her horns. "Horns grow the way they grow!" she remarked crossly. "So what are you going to do about it?"

"Something!" answered the young cow. "I'm not Wonderful-cow-that-never-was for nothing!" And she stopped having krink-kranks and went off. She stayed away all day and when she did come back, her horns were curled up tight! And she was chewing and smiling and chewing and smiling.

"What have you done now?" gasped the old

mother cow. "I never saw horns curled so crumply!"

The young cow smiled and said:

> "I'm a wonderful cow
> And I don't know how
> Such wonderful things I do!
> I curl my horn
> On the cob of a corn
> And smile whenever I chew,
> I do,
> I smile whenever I chew!"

"And here is the corn cob I curled them on," she said, opening her mouth. And sure enough, there was the corn cob!

Now Wonderful-cow-that-never-was got queerer and queerer until the farmer thought her a little *too* queer. She was very proud of her crumpled horns and tried to hook everyone on them. Once she tore the farmer's coat trying to hook him. And once she *did* toss him up. She watched him in the air and all she said was "He's up now, but he'll come down some time." And bang! So he did!

Finally one terrible day, they tied her tight and cut off her horns. She was never the same afterwards. She couldn't hook any more. "I don't

care about being queer any more," she said to her
mother. And she wasn't. She stopped standing
on her head. She never pulled off another ear.
She never broke her tail again and of course she
never curled her horns again. Because she hadn't
any! "After all," she said, "it's wonderful enough
just to be a cow and have four stomachs and chew
cud and give milk and have a baby each Spring!"
And that's what she's doing now!

> She's a wonderful cow,
> And anyhow
> She does a wonderful thing!
> She wallows in mud,
> She chews her cud,
> And has a baby in Spring!

THINGS THAT LOVED THE LAKE

This story was worked out with a five-year-old boy. It is the result of his own summer experiences on a lake.

THINGS THAT LOVED THE LAKE

Once there was a little lake. And many things loved the little lake for its water was clear and smooth and blue when it was sunshiny, and dark

and wavy and cross-looking when it was rainy. Now one of the things that loved the little lake was a little fish. He was a slippery shiny little fish all covered with slippery shiny scales. He

lived in the shadow of a big rock near a deep,
dark, cool pool. And when his wide-open shiny
eye saw a little fly fall on the top of the water, he
would flip his slippery, shiny tail and wave his
slippery, shiny fins and dart out and up and—snap!
he'd have the fly inside him! Then like a shiny
streak he'd quietly slip back to the cool, deep,
dark pool.

Another thing that loved the little lake was a
spotted green frog. He too lived near the big
rock. He would squat like a lump on the top in
the sun, blinking his bright little eyes. Then
splash! jump he would go, plump into the water.
He'd keep his funny head with the little blinking,
bright eyes above water while he'd kick his long,
spotted, green legs and he'd swim across to another rock. At first he used to frighten the slippery shiny little fish when he came tumbling into
the quiet water. But the spotted green frog never
did anything to hurt the little fish so the slippery
shiny little fish didn't mind him after all. But at
night what do you think the spotted green frog
did? He squatted on the rock with his front feet
toeing in, like this, and he looked up at the far-
away white moon in the far-away dark sky, and
then he swelled and he swelled and he swelled his
throat, and then he opened his wide, wide mouth

and out came a noise. Oh, such a noise! "K-K-K-Krink!! K-K-K-Krank!!" All night the spotted frog swelled his throat and croaked at the moon.

Now another thing that loved the little lake was a beautiful wild duck. The wild duck had beautiful green and brown feathers and on his head he had a little green top-knot. Every year he flew north from the warm south where he had been spending the winter. High up in the air he flew, leading many other beautiful wild ducks. He flew with his head stretched out and his feet tucked up close to his body and his strong wings flapping, flapping, flapping like great fans. And as he flew way up in the air his keen eye would see the little lake glistening down below. "Quonk-quonk!" he would call. And the other wild ducks would answer, "Quonk-quonk-quonk!" And then they would swoop, right down to the little lake and they'd light right on the water. There they would sit, rocking on the little waves or swimming about with their red webbed feet. Oh, the wild ducks loved the little lake very much!

But not the slippery shiny fish, not the spotted green frog, not the beautiful wild duck loves the lake as much as some one else does. I don't believe any one else loves the little lake as much as does the little summer boy! Sometimes

the little summer boy goes rowing on top of the
lake. He leans way forward and stretches his
oars way back, then he puts them into the water
and pulls as hard as ever he can—splash—splash
—splash—splash——! And the boat glides and
slides right over the water! Sometimes,—and this
he loves better still,—he stands on the rock in his
red bathing suit. Then plump! he jumps right
into the water! Sometimes he goes feetwards and
sometimes he goes headwards and sometimes he
turns a somersault in the air before he touches the
water. And then away he goes moving his arms
and kicking his legs almost like the spotted green
frog. But the little fish when he hears this great
thing come splashing into the quiet water, he flips
his slippery shiny tail and waves his slippery shiny
fins and darts way out into the deep water where
the little boy with the red bathing suit can't follow him. For to the little fish this little summer
boy seems very queer, and very, *very* noisy, and
very, *very*, VERY enormous! And the spotted green
frog too gets out of the way when the little boy
comes racketing into the water. He hops, hops
under the rocks into a safe little cave and from
there he watches and blinks his bright little eyes.
But he never croaks then! The little summer boy
knows the green frog is there and sometimes he

peeks at him and thinks "I wish I could make my back legs go like yours!" For he's often seen the spotted green frog swim from rock to rock.

But the beautiful wild duck, he never saw the little summer boy. For long before the boy came to the little lake, the duck had left the lake far behind. Early one morning in Spring he flapped his strong wings and tucked his wet webbed feet up close to his body and stretched out his long neck and calling "Quonk-quonk!" he flapped away to the north. And all the other beautiful wild ducks followed calling, "Quonk-quonk-quonk!" So the little summer boy never knew the wild duck!

It is too bad that the fish and the frog are scared away when the summer boy goes in bathing. But it is only for a little while anyway. For the little summer boy's mother doesn't let him play in the lake all day as does the mother of the slippery shiny fish and the mother of the spotted green frog. She has called him now, and he calls back, "One more time!" for no one loves the little lake as much as the little boy in the red bathing suit. He has climbed up on the rock. The water is running down him, for he is as wet as a baby seal. Now he puts out his hands, like this, and he calls out, "This time I'm going to take a headwards dive!"

In the lake they play,
The spotted green frog
And the slippery shiny fish.
They frisk and they whisk,
And they dip and they flip.
And the water it glimmers,
It ripples and twinkles
When the frog and the fishes play.

In the lake they play,
The beautiful duck
And the rackety summer boy.
When the wild duck swims
The water it skims.
But the boy with a shout
He plumps in, he jumps out.
And the little lake shakes with his play.

HOW THE SINGING WATER
GOT TO THE TUB

In this story I have tried to make the refrains carry the essential points in the content. I have tried, however, to subordinate the information to the pattern. This story came in response to direct questions during baths.

HOW THE SINGING WATER GOT TO THE TUB

Once there was a little singing stream of water. It sang whatever it did. And it did many things from the time it bubbled up in the far-away hills to the time it splashed into the dirty little boy's tub. It began as a little spring of water. Then the water was as cool as cool could be for it came up from the deep cool earth all hidden away from the sun. It came up into a little hollow scooped out of the earth and in the hollow were little pebbles. Right up through the pebbles, bubbling and gurgling it came. And what do you suppose the water did when the little hollow was all full? It did just what water always does, it tried to find a way to run down hill! One side of the little hollow was lower than the others and here the water spilled over and trickled down. And this is the song the water sang then:

> "I bubble up so cool
> Into the pebbly pool.
> Over the edge I spill
> And gallop down the hill!"

So the water became a little stream and began its long journey to the little boy's tub. And always it wanted to run down—always down, and as it ran, it tinkled this song:

> "I sing, I run,
> In the shade, in the sun,
> It's always fun
> To sing and to run.'

Sometimes it pushed under twigs and leaves; sometimes it made a big noise tumbling over the roots of trees; sometimes it flowed all quiet and slow through long grasses in a meadow. Once it came to the edge of a pretty big rock and over it went, splashing and crashing and dashing and making a fine, fine spray.

It sang to the little birds that took their baths in the spray. And the little birds ruffled their feathers to get dry and sang back to the little brook. "Ching-a-reel" they sang. It sang to the bunny rabbit who got his whiskers all wet when he took a drink. It sang to the mother deer who always came to the same place and licked up some water with her tongue. To all of these and many more little wild wood things the little brook rippled its song:

> "I sing, I run,
> In the shade, in the sun,
> It's always fun
> To sing and to run."

But to the fish in the big dark pool under the rocks it sang so softly, so quietly, that only the fishes heard.

Now all the time that the little brook kept running down hill, it kept getting bigger. For every once in a while it would be joined by another little brook coming from another hillside spring. And, of course, the two of them were twice as large as each had been alone. This kept happening until the stream was a small river,—so big and deep that the horses couldn't ford it any more. Then people built bridges over it, and this made the small river feel proud. Little boats sailed in it too,—canoes and sail boats and row boats. Sometimes they held a lot of little boys without any clothes on who jumped into the water and splashed and laughed and splashed and laughed.

At last the river was strong enough to carry great gliding boats, with deep deep voices. "Toot," said the boats, "tootoot-tooooooooot!"

And now the song of the river was low and slow as it answered the song of the boats:

"I grow and I flow
As I carry the boats,
As I carry the boats of men."

After the little river had been running down
hill for ever so long, it came to a place where the
banks went up very high and steep on each side
of it. Here something strange happened. The
little river was stopped by an enormous wall. The
wall was made of stone and cement and it stretched
right across the river from one bank to the other.
The little river couldn't get through the wall, so
it just filled up behind it. It filled and filled until
it found that it had spread out into a real little
lake. Only the people who walked around it
called it a reservoir!

Now in the wall was just one opening down
near the bottom. And what do you suppose that
led to? A pipe! But the pipe was so big that
an elephant could have walked down it swinging
his trunk! Only, of course, there wasn't any elephant there.

Now the little river didn't like to have his race
down hill stopped. So he began muttering to
himself:

"What shall I do, oh, what shall I do?
Here's a big dam and I can't get through!

Behind the dam I fill and fill
But I want to go running and running down hill!
If the pipe at the bottom will let me through
I'll run through the pipe! That's what I'll do!"

So he rushed into the pipe as fast as he could
for there he found he could run down hill again!
He ran and he ran for miles and miles. Above
him he knew there were green fields and trees and
cows and horses. These were the things he had
sung to before he rushed into the pipe. Then
after a long time he knew he was under something
different. He could feel thousands of feet scurry-
ing this way and that; he could feel thousands of
horses pulling carriages and wagons and trucks;
he could feel cars, subways, engines;—he could
feel so many things crossing him that he wondered
they didn't all bump each other. Then he knew
he was under the Big City. And this is the song
he shouted then:

"Way under the street, street, street,
I feel the feet, feet, feet.
I feel their beat, beat, beat,
Above on the street, street, street."

And then again something queer happened.
Every once in a while a pipe would go off from
the big pipe. Now one of these pipes turned into

a certain street and then a still smaller pipe turned off into a certain house and a still smaller pipe went right up between the walls of the house. And in this house there lived the dirty little boy.

The water flowed into the street pipe and then it flowed into the house pipe and then,—what do

you think?—it went right up that pipe between the walls of the house! For you see even the top of that dirty little boy's house isn't nearly as high as the reservoir on the hill where the water started and the water can run up just as high as it has run down.

In the bathroom was the dirty little boy. His face was dirty, his hands were dirty, his feet were dirty and his knees—oh! his knees were very, very dirty. This very dirty little boy went over to the faucet and slowly turned it. Out came the water splashing, and crashing and dashing.

"My! but I need a bath tonight," said the dirty little boy as he heard the water splashing in the tub. The water was still the singing water that had sung all the way from the far-away hills. It had sung a bubbling song when it gurgled up as a spring; it had sung a tinkling song as it rippled down hill as a brook; it had crooned a flowing song when it bore the talking boats; it had muttered and throbbed and sung to itself as it ran through the big, big pipe. Now as it splashed into the dirty little boy's tub it laughed and sang this last song:

> "I run from the hill,—down, down, down,
> Under the streets of the town, town, town,
> Then in the pipe, up, up, up,
> I tumble right into your tub, tub, tub."

And the dirty little boy laughed and jumped into the Singing Water!

THE CHILDREN'S NEW DRESSES

An old pattern with new content. The steps in the process were originally dug out by a child of six through his own questions.

THE CHILDREN'S NEW DRESSES

Once there was a small town. In the small town were many houses and in the houses were many people. In one of these houses there lived a mother with a great many children. One night after the children were all in bed and the mother was sitting by the fire, a brick fell down the chimney. Then another came bumping and rattling down. Now outside there was a great wind blowing. It whistled down the chimney and up flamed the fire. The sparks flew into the hole where the bricks had fallen out. The first thing the mother knew the house was all on fire. Still the great wind roared. The house next door caught fire, then the next, then the next, then the next, until half the little town was burning. The mother with the many children and many other frightened people ran to the part of the town behind the great wind. And there they stayed until the wind died down and they could put the fire out.

Now many of these people's clothes had burned with their houses. The many children who had gone to bed before the fire began had nothing

to wear except their nightclothes. The mother
went to the store. That too was burned! But she
found the storekeeper and said:—"Storekeeper,

sell me some dresses for my children for their
dresses have been burned and they have nothing
to wear."

"But, mother of the many children," the storekeeper replied, "first I must get me the dresses.
For that I must send to the many-fingered factory
in the middle of the city."

So he sent to the many-fingered factory in the
middle of the great city and he said:—"Clothier,
send me some dresses that I may sell to the mother;

for her children's dresses have burned up and they have nothing to wear."

But the clothier in the many-fingered factory replied:—"First I must get me the cloth. For that I must send to the weaving mill. The weaving mill is in the hills where there is water to turn its wheels."

So the clothier sent to the weaving mill in the hills where there is water to turn its wheels and said:—"Weaver, send me the cloth that the many fingers at the factory may make dresses to send to the storekeeper in the small town to sell to the mother; for her children's dresses have burned up and they have nothing to wear."

But the weaver in the weaving mill in the hills sent back word:—"First I must get me the cotton. For that I must send to the cotton fields. The cotton fields are in the south where the land is hot and low."

So the weaver in the weaving mill in the hills sent to the cotton plantation, and he said:— "Planter, send me the cotton from the hot low lands that I may make cloth in the mill in the hills to send to the clothier in the many-fingered factory in the middle of the great city to be made into dresses to send to the storekeeper in the small town to sell to the mother; for her children's dresses have burned up and they have nothing to wear."

But the planter sent back word:—"First I must get the negroes to pick the cotton. For cotton

must be picked in the hot sun and negroes are the only ones who can stand the sun."

So the planter went to the negroes and he said:—"Pick me the cotton from the hot low lands that I may send it to the weaver in his mill in the hills that he may weave the cloth to send to the clothier in the many-fingered factory in the middle of the great city to make dresses to send to the storekeeper in the small town to sell to the mother;

for her children's dresses have burned up and they
have nothing to wear."

But the negroes answered:—"First de sun, he
hab got to shine and shine and shine! 'Cause de
sun, he am de only one dat can make dem little
seed bolls bust wide open!"

So the negroes sang to the sun:—"Big sun, so
shiny hot! Is you gwine to shine on dem cotton
bolls so we can pick de cotton for de massah so
he can send it to de weaver in de weaving mills
in de hills to weave into cloth so he can send it
to de clothier in de many-fingered factory in de
middle of de big city to make dresses to send to
de storekeeper in de small town so he can sell it
to de mammy; for de chillun's dresses hab gone
and burned up and dey ain't got nothin' to wear!"

Now the sun heard the song of the negroes of the
south. And he began to shine. And he kept on
shining on the hot low lands. And when the cotton
bolls on the hot low lands felt the sun shine and
shine and shine, they burst wide open. Then the
negroes picked the cotton, the planter shipped it,
the weaver wove it, the clothier made it into dresses, and the storekeeper sold them to the mother.

So at last the many children took off their nightclothes and put on their new dresses. And so
they were all happy again!

OLD DAN GETS THE COAL

The occupations of the city horse are always absorbing to the school children. They have many tales about various "Old Dans" and their various trades. The docks are familiar to almost all the children,—even to the four-year-olds. This verse is meant to be read fast or slow according to whether or no the wagon is empty.

OLD DAN GETS THE COAL

Old Dan, he lives in a stable, he does,
He sleeps in a stable stall.
Old Dan, he eats in the stable, he does,
He eats the hay from the manger, he does,
    He pulls the hay
    And he chews the hay
When he eats in his stable stall.

Old Dan, he leaves the stable, he does,
He pulls the wagon behind.
Old Dan he goes trotting along, so he does,
He trots with the wagon all empty, he does;
    The wagon, it clatters,
    The mud, it all spatters
Old Dan with the wagon behind.

Old Dan, he trots to the dock, he does,
He trots to the coal barge dock.
Old Dan, he stands by the barge, he does,
He stands and the big crane creaks, it does.
    Up! into the chute,
    Bang! out of the chute
Comes the coal at the coal barge dock!

Old Dan, he pulls the load, he does,
He pulls the heavy load.

Old Dan he pulls the coal, he does,
He slowly pulls the heavy coal.
   The wagon thumps,
   It bumps, it clumps
When old Dan pulls the load.

Old Dan, he stands by the house, he does,
And the coal rattles out behind.
Old Dan stands still by the house, he does,
He stands and the slippery coal, so it does
   Goes rattlety klang!
   Zippy kabang!
As it slides from the wagon behind!

Old Dan, he then leaves the house, so he does,
A-pulling the wagon behind.
Old Dan he goes trotting along, so he does,
He trots with the wagon all empty, he does.
   The wagon it clatters,
   The mud it all spatters
Old Dan with the wagon behind.

Old Dan, comes home to his stable, he does,
Home to his stable stall.
He finds the hay in the stable, he does,
He eats the hay from the manger, he does,
   He pulls the hay,
   He chews the hay,
Then he sleeps in his stable stall.

THE SUBWAY CAR

The relationship which this story aims to clarify is the social significance of the subway car—its construction and the need it answers to. Children have enjoyed the verse better, I think, than any other in the book.

THE SUBWAY CAR

The surface car is a poky car,
It stops 'most every minute.
At every corner someone gets out
And someone else gets in it.

It stops for a lady, an auto, a hoss,
For any old thing that wants to cross,
This poky old, stupid old, silly old, timid old,
      lumbering surface car.

Up on high against the sky
The elevated train goes by.
Above it soars, above it roars
On level with the second floors
Of dirty houses, dirty stores
Who have to see, who have to hear
This noisy ugly monster near.
And as it passes hear it yell,
"I'm the deafening, deadening, thunderous,
        hideous, competent, elegant el."

Under the ground like a mole in a hole,
I tear through the white tiled tunnel,
With my wire brush on the rail I rush
From station to lighted station.
Levers pull, the doors fly ope',
People press against the rope.
And some are stout and some are thin
And some get out and some get in.
Again I go. Beginning slow
I race, I chase at a terrible pace,
I flash and I dash with never a crash,
I hurry, I scurry with never a flurry.
I tear along, flare along, singing my lightning
        song,
"I'm the rushing, speeding, racing, fleeting, rapid
        subway car."

THE SUBWAY CAR

Whew-ee-ee-ee-ew-ew went the siren whistle. And all the men and all the women hurried toward the factory. For that meant it was time to begin work. Each man and each woman went to his particular machine. The steam was up; the belts were moving; the wheels were whirring; the piston rods were shooting back and forth. And one man made a piece of wheel, and one man made a part of a brake, and one man made a belt, and one man made a leather strap, and one man made a door, and one man made some straw-covered seats, and one man made a window-frame, and one man made a little wire brush. And then some other men took all these things and began putting them together. And when the car was finished some other men came and painted it, and on the side they painted the number 793.

The car stood on the siding wondering what he was for and what he was to do. Suddenly he heard another car come bumping and screeching down the track. Before the new car could think what was happening,—bang!—the battered old car went smash into him. This seemed to be just what the man standing along side expected. For the car felt him swing on to the steps and shout "Go

ahead." At the same minute the car felt a piece
of iron slip from his own rear and hook into the
front of the other car.

And "go ahead" he did, though No. 793 thought
he would be wrenched to pieces.

"Whatever is happening to me?" he nervously
asked the car that was pushing him. "I feel my
wheels going round and round underneath me and
I can't stop them. Can't you just hear me creak?
I'm afraid I will split in two."

The dilapidated old thing behind simply
screamed with delight as he jounced over a switch.

"See here, now," he said in a rasping voice,
"what do you think wheels are for anyway if they
are not to go round? And if you can't hang together in a quiet little jaunt like this, you had
better turn into a baby carriage and be done with
it. Say, what do you think you were made for
anyway, Freshie?"

With this he gave a vicious pull. Freshie
thought it would probably loosen every carefully
fastened bolt in his whole structure.

"And what's more," continued the amused and
irritated old car, "if you think all you've got to
do is to be pulled around like a fine lady in a
limousine, you are pretty well fooled. Wait till

you feel the juice go through you—just wait—
that's all I say."

"What is juice?" groaned No. 793.

But he could get no answer except "Just wait,
you will find out soon enough."

In another minute he had found out. He felt
his door pulled open and a heavy tread come
clump, clump, clump down the whole length of
him to the little closet room at the end. There
he felt levers pulled and switches turned. Suddenly the little wire brush underneath him
dropped until it touched the third rail. Z-z-zr-
zr-zr-zz-zz—What in the name of all blazes was
happening to him? He tingled in every bolt. He
quivered with fear. "This must be the juice!"
Another lever was turned. He leaped forward
on the track, jerking and thumping and creaking.

Then he settled down and it wasn't so bad. The
first scare was over. He did not go to pieces. On
the contrary he felt so excited and strong that he
almost told the old thing behind him to take off
his brush and let himself be pulled. But he was
afraid of the cross old car. So he ventured
timidly: "Isn't this great? I should like to go
flying along in the sun like this all day."

"In the sun?" snarled his old companion.

"Come now, Freshie, can't you catch on to what you are? You just look your fill at the old sun now for you won't see him again for some time."

"Why not?" whimpered No. 793.

But he needed no answer. Ahead of him he could see the track sliding down into a deep hole. The earth closed over him in a queer rounded arch, all lined with shiny white tiles. At the same moment the lights all up and down his own ceiling flashed on. He noticed then that he had a red lantern on his front. He could tell it by the red, glinting reflections it threw on the tiles as he tore along. Ahead he could see a great cluster of lights which seemed to be rushing towards him. Of course he was really rushing towards them, but he was so excited he got all mixed in his ideas.

"Where are we? And what on earth is that rushing towards us? And why do we come down here under the ground?" he screamed to the old car behind.

"There's no room for us on top," jerked the old car. "There are a heap of people in this old city of New York, Freshie, and you will find 'em on the surface or scooting in the elevated and here jogging along underneath the earth."

"People!" screamed No. 793, "I don't see any. What do we do with them in this hole anyway?"

Even as he spoke he felt the man in the little closet room in his front turn something. His wire brush lifted and all his strength seemed to ooze away. Then something clutched his wheels. He screeched,—yes, he really screeched, and then he stood still, close to the station platform. The station looked big to No. 793 and very brilliantly lighted. It was jammed with people who stood pressed against ropes in long rows.

A man on his own platform pulled down a handle and then another. He felt his end doors and then his center doors fly open. Then tramp, tramp, tramp, tramp—a hundred feet came pounding on his floor. He could feel them and somehow he liked the feel. He could even feel two small feet that walked much faster than the others, and in another moment he felt two little knees on one of his straw-covered seats. Then the handles were pulled again. His doors banged closed; z-zr-zr-rr—the brush underneath touched the rail and the electricity shot through him. He felt a hundred feet shift quickly and heavily. He felt his leather straps clutched by a hundred hands. And amid the noise he heard a little voice say, "Father, isn't this a brand new subway car?" And then he knew what he was!

BORIS TAKES A WALK AND FINDS
MANY DIFFERENT KINDS OF TRAINS

This first story is an attempt to let a child discover
the significance of his every-day environment,—of
subways and elevated railways. Here there is no
content new to the city child. But the relationship
to congestion he has not always seen for himself. In
the second story the lay-out of New York on a
crowded island is discovered. Again the content is
old but its significance may be new. Both these stories
verge on the informational.

BORIS TAKES A WALK AND FINDS MANY DIFFERENT KINDS OF TRAINS

> Many little boys and girls
> With fathers and with mothers,
> Many little boys and girls
> With sisters and with brothers,
> Many little boys and girls
> They come from far away.
> They sail and sail to big New York,
> And there they land and stay!
> And you would never, never guess
> When they grow big and tall,
> That they had come from far away
> When they were wee and small!

One of the little boys who sailed and sailed until he came to big New York was named Boris. He came as the others did, with his father and his mother and his sisters and his brothers. He came from a wide green country called Russia. In that country he had never seen a city, never seen wharves with ocean steamers and ferry boats and tug boats and barges,—never seen a street so crowded you could hardly get through, had never

seen great high buildings reaching up, up, up
to the clouds, he thought.   And he had never heard
a city, never heard the noise of elevated trains and
surface cars and automobiles and the many, many
hurrying feet.   He often thought of the wide green
country he had left behind, and he used to talk

about it to his mother in a funny language you
wouldn't understand.   For Boris and his family
still spoke Russian.   But Boris was nine years old
and he loved new things as well as old.   So he
grew to love this crowded noisy new home of his
as well as the still wide country he had left.

Now Boris had been in New York quite a while.

But he hadn't been out on the streets much. One day he said to his mother in the funny language, "I think I'll take a walk!"

"All right," she answered, "be careful you don't get run over by one of those queer wagons that run without horses!"

"Yes I will," laughed Boris for he was a careful and a smart little boy and knew well how to take care of himself for all he was so little.

So Boris went out on the street. He walked to the corner and waited to go across.

Kachunk, kachunk, kachunk went by an auto;
Clopperty, clopperty, clopperty went by a horse;
Thunk-a-ta, thunk-a-ta, bang, bang went by a truck.

He waited another minute.

Kachunk, kachunk, kachunk went by an auto;
Clopperty, clopperty, clopperty went by a horse;
Thunk-a-ta, thunk-a-ta, bang, bang went by a truck.

He stood there a long while watching this stream of autos and horses and trucks go by and he thought:

"Dear me! dear me!
What shall I do?
The're so many things,
I'll never get through!"

Just then all the autos and the horses and the

trucks stopped. They stood still right in front of
him. And Boris saw that the big man standing
in the middle of the street had put up his hand to

stop them. So he scampered across. Boris didn't
know that the big man was the traffic policeman!

Now Boris scampered down the block to the
next street. There he waited to go across.

Kachunk, kachunk, kachunk went by an auto;
Clopperty, clopperty, clopperty went by a horse;
Thunk-a-ta, thunk-a-ta, bang, bang went by a truck.

He stood there a long time watching the autos
and horses and trucks go by. And he thought:

"Dear me! dear me!
What shall I do?
The're so many things,
I'll never get through!"

Boris looked at the big policeman who stood in the middle of *this* street. After a while the big policeman raised his hand and all the autos and horses and trucks stopped and Boris scampered across and ran down the block to the next street crossing. And there the same thing happened again.

Kachunk, kachunk, kachunk went by an auto;
Clopperty, clopperty, clopperty went by a horse;
Thunk-a-ta, thunk-a-ta, bang, bang went by a truck.

"I'll not get much of a walk this way," he thought. "I have to wait and wait at each corner. And the're so many things I'll never get through." Just then he saw a street car. "I might take a car," he thought. But then he saw on the street a long line of cars waiting, waiting to get through. "It wouldn't do much good", he thought. "They're just like me."

"Dear me! dear me!
What can they do?
The're so many things,
They'll never get through!"

Then he noticed a big hole in the sidewalk.
Down the hole went some steps and down the steps
hurried lots and lots of people. "I wonder what
this is?" thought Boris and down the steps he ran.

At the bottom of the steps there was a big room
all lined with white tile and all lighted with electric lights. On the side was the funniest little
house with a little window in it and a man looking
through the window. Boris watched carefully for

he didn't understand. Everyone went up to the window and gave the man 5 cents and the man handed out a little piece of blue paper.

"That's a ticket," thought Boris, for he was a very smart little boy. "These people must be going somewhere." So he reached down in his pocket and pulled out a nickel. For all he was so little, and so new to New York, he knew what a 5 cent piece was quite well. He had to stand on tiptoe to hand the man his nickel and to reach his little blue ticket. Then he watched again. Everyone dropped this ticket in a funny little box by a funny little gate and another man moved a handle up and down. So Boris did just the same. He stood on tiptoe and dropped his ticket in the box and walked through the little gate to a big platform. And what do you think he saw there? A great long tunnel stretching off in both directions,—a long tunnel all lined with white tiles! And on the bottom were rails! "I wonder what runs on that track?" thought Boris.

Just then he heard a most terrible noise:

Rackety, clackety, klang, klong!
Rackety, clackety, klang, klong!

and down the tunnel came a train of cars. "Yi-i-i-i—sh-sh-sh-sh!" screamed the cars and stopped right in front of Boris. And then what do you suppose happened? The doors in the car right in front of him flew open. Everyone stepped in. So did Boris.

It was the front car. He walked to the front and sat down where he could look out on the tracks. He could also look into the funny little box room and see the man who pulled the levers and made the car go and stop. In a moment they started:

> Rackety, clackety, klang, klong!
> How fast! How fast!

Then "Yi-i-i-i—sh-sh-sh-sh!" The man put on the brakes and they stopped at another station. In another moment they started again. Rackety, clackety, klang, klong! Then "Yi-i-i-i—sh-sh-sh-sh" another station! And so they went flying from lighted station to lighted station through the white-tiled tunnel.

Boris was very happy. He sat quite still watching out of the window and saying with the car; rackety, clackety, klang, klong; rackety, clackety, klang, klong! "This is the way to go if you're in a hurry," he thought. He looked up and smiled to think of all the autos and horses and trucks above going oh! so slowly down the street!

At last he thought he would get out. So the next time the man put the brakes on and the train yelled "Yi-i-i-i—sh-sh-sh-sh!" Boris walked through the open doors on to the platform, then through the little gate, up some long steps and found himself on the street again. But right near him what do you think he saw? A park all full of trees and grass! This made Boris happy for he hadn't seen so many trees and so much grass since he had left the wide country in his old home in Russia. A little breeze was blowing too! He clapped his hands and ran around and laughed and laughed and laughed and sang:

> "I like the grass,
> I like the trees,
> I like the sky,
> I like the breeze!
> I touch the grass,
> I touch the trees,
> Let me play in the Park,
> Oh, please! oh, please!"

So he ran all round and played in the Park.

Suddenly he thought it was time to go home. He looked for the hole in the sidewalk but he couldn't find it. And he didn't know how to ask for the subway for he didn't know its name and he couldn't talk English. "I'll have to walk!" he thought. He knew he must walk south for he had noticed which way the sun was when he went into the hole in the sidewalk. And now he noticed again where it was and so he could tell which way was south.

So Boris went out on the street. He walked to the corner and waited to go across.

Kachunk, kachunk, kachunk went by an auto;
Clopperty, clopperty, clopperty went by a horse,
Thunk-a-ta, thunk-a-ta, bang, bang went by a truck.

He waited another minute.

Kachunk, kachunk, kachunk went by an auto;
Clopperty, clopperty, clopperty went by a horse;
Thunk-a-ta, thunk-a-ta, bang, bang went by a truck.

He stood there a long time watching the stream of autos and horses and trucks go by. And he thought; "I'll never get home if I have to go as slowly as this.

"Dear me! dear me!
What shall I do?
The're so many things
I'll never get through!"

And for all he was so smart he was a very little boy and he began to cry for his legs were tired and he was a little frightened, too.

Just then what do you suppose he saw? Down the street way up in the air on a kind of trestle, he saw a train of cars tearing by. "That's just what I want! That train doesn't have to stop for autos and horses and things!" thought Boris and he ran down the street. When he got to the high trestle, there was a long flight of stairs. Up the steps went Boris. At the top he found another funny little room with a window in it and a man looking out. This time he knew just what to do. He stood on tiptoe and gave the man 5 cents and the man handed him a little red piece of paper. Boris took it, walked through a little gate, stood on tiptoe and dropped the ticket into another funny little box and another man moved the handle up and down and his ticket dropped down. And what do you suppose he saw from the platform? Tracks again! Tracks stretching out in both directions. He didn't have to wait on the platform long before he heard the train coming. It seemed to say:

"I'm the elevated train, I'm the elevated train, I'm the elevated, elevated, elevated train!" It stopped right in front of Boris and Boris got into the front car again. Here was another man in another little box room moving more levers and making this train stop and go. And Boris could look right out in front and see the stations before he reached them. He could see bridges before they tore under them; he could look down and see the horses and the autos and the trucks. He smiled as he saw how slowly they had to go while he was racing along above them.

So Boris was quite happy and sat very still and watched out of the window. Suddenly he heard the conductor call "Fourteenth Street!" Now that was one of the few English words that Boris knew for he lived on 14th Street. Now he was pleased for he knew he was near home. So he got off the car, ran down the long, long steps and found himself on the street. Down 14th Street he ran until he came to his house.

"Well," called his mother. "You've been gone a long time! What did you see on the streets?"

Boris smiled. "I haven't been *on* the streets much mother."

His mother was surprised. "Where have you been if you haven't been on the streets?" she asked.

Boris laughed and laughed. "There were so many things on the streets, so many autos and horses and trucks," he said, "that I couldn't go fast. So I found a wonderful train *under* the streets and I went out on that. And I found a wonderful train *over* the streets and I came home on that!"

"Well, well," said his mother. "Trains under
and trains over! Think of that!" And Boris did
think of them much. And when he was in bed
that night, he seemed to hear this little song about
them:

> "Now out on the streets
> There everything meets
> And they're all in a hurry to go.
>   But what can they do
>   For they can't get through
> And all are so terribly slow?
>
> "But under the street
> Where nothing can meet
> The subway goes rackety, klack!
>   It can dash and can race,
>   It can flash and can chase,
> For there's nothing ahead on the track.
>
> "And over the street
> Where nothing can meet
> Is a wonderful train indeed!
>   High up the stair
>   Way up in the air
> It goes at remarkable speed."

BORIS WALKS EVERY WAY IN NEW YORK

PART 1

One morning when Boris was eating his breakfast, he suddenly thought of the wide green country around his old home in Russia. I don't know what made him think of it. He just did! "Mother," he said, "I want to see some grass."

His mother smiled. "Want to go to the Park, Boris?" she asked.

"No, more grass than that even. I want to see it everywhere," and Boris waved his arms around. "I think I'll go and find lots and lots of it!"

"I'd like to see lots and lots of grass too, Boris," smiled his mother. But her eyes were full of tears too! "But I don't know where you can go in New York and see grass everywhere!"

"Then I'll go out of New York!" cried Boris. "If I walk far enough I'll surely find grass, won't I?"

"You can try," answered his mother. Boris was now much bigger than when he came to New

York and could talk quite a little English too. So his mother let him walk over the city alone. Boris clapped his hands! For though he was much bigger, he was still a little boy, you know!

"Which way had I better go?" thought Boris when he was out on the street. "I think I'll go west first." So he walked west. Though the streets were crowded he had learned to go faster than when he took his first walk and discovered the subway and elevated. West, west, west he went. Street after street,—houses set close together all the way. Then at last he saw something that made him run. The city came to an end! And there was a big river, oh! such an enormous river! The edge of the river was all docks,— docks as far as he could look. Across on the other side he could see another city with big chimneys and lots and lots of smoke. There were lots of boats in the river too. "Some day I'll come and watch them," thought Boris excitedly, "but now I want to find my grass." So he turned around. "I'll have to go east, I guess," he thought.

So east he went. East he went until he came to his house. But he did not stop. He went right by it. "How many houses there are" he thought. "How many people there must be!" And still he walked east. And still the houses were set close together street after street. After a while he saw something that made him run again. The city came to an end! And there was another big river! This edge too was all docks,—docks as far as he could look. Across on the other side he could see another city with big chimneys and lots of smoke. "Well," thought Boris, "isn't it the funniest thing that when I walk west I come to a river and when I walk east I come to a river too!"

Now this puzzled him so that he thought he must ask somebody about it. Close to him was a big dock and at the dock was a flat barge. A lot of men were unloading coal from her. He walked up to one. "Please," he said, "what river is this?"

The man stopped his work for a minute. "It's the East River of course. Where do you come from, boy?"

"From Russia," said Boris, "so you see I didn't know. And please, is the other river the West River then?"

"What other river, boy? What are you talking about?"

This made Boris feel very uncomfortable, but he knew there was another river in the west for hadn't he just walked there? So he said bravely,

"If you keep walking west you *do* come to another river. I know you do! For I've done it. And it's a bigger river than this, too!"

The man laughed out loud. "Right you are, boy!" he said. "You're a great walker, you are. Did you walk all the way from Russia?" Now Boris thought the man couldn't know very much to ask him such a question. But, then, he didn't know much either. He was asking questions too! So he answered, "Oh! no! I came on an enormous boat. But please you haven't told me the name of the other river?"

The man laughed louder than ever. "It's a funny thing, boy, that we call it the North River. But you are right: it *is* west! It's really the Hudson River, boy, that's what it is. And a mighty big river it is too. Want to know anything more?" And the man turned back to his work.

"Well," thought Boris. "I can't get to my grass today if I strike rivers everywhere I go." And he turned and walked home slowly, because he was sorry. And he was very, very tired too. For you see he had walked all the way across the city twice and that is a pretty long walk even for a boy the size of Boris.

Boris, he went out to walk
To find the country wide.
And he walked west and west he walked
But found the Hudson wide!
And so he turned himself about
And walked the other way
And he walked east and east he walked
And there East River lay!

PART 2

The next morning at breakfast, Boris suddenly thought again of the wide green country around his old home in Russia. I don't know why he thought of it again. He just did! And then he thought of the Hudson River he had found by walking west and of the East River he had found by walking east. "I might try walking north this time," he thought. And so he said to his mother, "I think I'll go on another hunt for grass,—grass that's everywhere!" and again he waved his arms.

"All right," answered his mother. "But I'm afraid you'll have to walk a long way to find grass everywhere!"

Out on the street he began to walk north. Then he remembered what a long long ride north in the subway he had had the other day. "I'd better take something if I want to get to the country wide," he thought.

So Boris went down to the subway and took the train. He rode for ever and ever so long. He kept wondering if there were still houses above him or if it was all grass,—lots and lots of grass. "I guess I'll go up and see," he thought. So up he went at the next station. But there were still houses everywhere. They weren't so high nor quite so close together; but still there was no grass. So he kept on walking north. Then he saw something that made him run. He could hardly believe his eyes. There was *another river!* "Oh! dear! oh! dear!" thought Boris. "I'll never in the world find the country wide if I strike a river whatever way I go. I think I'll take the subway and go way, way south. Surely I can get through that way. West a river, east a river, north a river. Yes, I'll go south!"

So again Boris went down to the subway and took a train going south. He stayed on it so long that he thought he must surely be way out in the country wide under grass, grass, everywhere. "I guess I'll go up and see," he thought.

So up he went at the next station. But when he came up he found himself on a street. There were high buildings all around him. He began to walk south. The farther he walked, the higher the buildings he found. At last he came to a place where the buildings reached up, up, up,—up to the clouds, he thought. He threw back his head to look at them,—so high above him that it made him almost dizzy to look at their tops. He wasn't sure they weren't going to fall either! Then he

looked down again. And what did he see at the end of the street? Trees, yes, green trees! "Perhaps I am coming to the wide green country," he thought. And he hurried on.

But when he got to the trees he saw that the city came to an end again. And what a wonderful end it was too! All around him was water,—water so full of boats that it made Boris gasp. When he looked to the west he could see a great river with another city on the other side. "That's the Hudson," thought Boris for he remembered what the coal man had told him. When he looked to the east he could see another great river. "That's the East River," he thought for he remembered that name too.

But what river was that out in front of him? Then suddenly Boris remembered. That was New York Harbor! This was where he had landed when he had come in the giant steamer from Russia! Out there was Ellis Island where he had stayed with his father and his mother and his sisters and his brothers until they had been looked at! He thought he could see Ellis Island from where he stood. But there were so many islands he couldn't be sure. But he *could* see the Statue of Liberty, that enormous woman holding a torch in her hand. He was sure of that. And he could see the boats everywhere all over the harbor. Boris stood there some time just staring and listening and staring.

When Boris he went out again
To find the country wide
And he went north and north he went
To Harlem River's side.

Again he turned himself about
And went the other way
And he went south and south he went
And there the harbor lay!

PART 3

Suddenly Boris remembered what he had come
for. He was looking for the wide green country,
for a place where grass grew everywhere. "This
is the funniest thing in the world," he thought,
scratching his head. "Wherever I walk in New
York I come to water. So many people and water
on every side of them! How do they ever get
out?" As soon as he thought of this, he began to
look around. Across the East River he could see
a giant bridge leaping from New York over to
another city and on the bridge were trains and cars
shooting back and forth and autos and horses and
people. "So that is the way they get out!" he
thought.

Then he looked to the west, to the Hudson
River. "No bridges there!" he said. "It's too

wide." Then he suddenly remembered the ferry
boat that had brought him from Ellis Island.
"Ferry boats, of course," he thought. And sure
enough there were ferry boats and ferry boats
going back and forth from New York to the other
side and to the little islands out in the harbor too!

Now Boris walked along thinking hard about
all this water all around New York. Just then he
noticed a lot of people coming up out of a hole in
the sidewalk. "The Subway," he thought, for you
remember he had been on the subway. But the
name over the steps didn't spell "subway." He
looked at it for a long time. At last he could read
it. "Hudson Tubes" it said. Hudson Tubes?
What could that mean? Boris wanted to know.
So he walked right up to a woman coming out
of the hole.

"What are the Hudson Tubes and where do
they take you?" he asked.

The woman laughed. "They take you to New
Jersey, of course," she said.

"Is that over there?" Boris asked, pointing
across the Hudson. "And do they really go under
the Hudson River?"

"Yes, to be sure they do. Where do you want
to go?" she answered and then Boris remembered
what he had been hunting for. "I want to go to

a wide green country where there is grass everywhere. But every way I walk in New York I
come to water. I know because I've walked east
and I've walked west and I've walked north and
I've walked south," he said, feeling a little like
crying for he was very tired and he *was* only a
little boy too. The woman smiled and she looked
nice when she smiled. "You see, boy," she said,
"New York is an island, so of course, you come
to water every way you walk. And it's so full
of people that there isn't any wide green country left,—except the Parks of course."

"Yes, I know the Parks," said Boris, "but that
isn't quite what I mean!"

The woman smiled again. "There *is* a wide
green country when you get out of the island," she
said. "You'll find it some day I'm sure," and then
the woman hurried away. Boris was very, very
tired. So he took the subway home. When he
came in his mother called out, "Did you find the
wide green country, Boris?"

"No," said Boris, "I couldn't, you see. Because
what do you think New York is?"

"What do I think New York is, Boris? Why,
it's the biggest city in the world!"

"That's not what I mean. What do you think
it *is?* What is it built on I mean?"

"What is it built on? On good sound rock I suppose!"

Boris laughed and laughed. "No, no," he said. "I mean it's an island. Every way you walk, if you walk long enough, you come to water. Now isn't that the funniest thing?" And Boris's mother thought it was funny too.

"So many people and all to live on an island!" she kept saying to herself. "I should think it would make them a lot of work!"

And Boris who remembered the bridges and the ferry boats and the "tubes" thought so too!

> Boris, he went out to walk
>   To find the country wide
> And he walked west and west he walked
>   But he found the Hudson wide!
> And so he turned himself about
>   And walked the other way
> And he walked east and east he walked
>   And there East River lay!
>
> But Boris he went out again
>   To find the country wide
> And he went north and north he went
>   To Harlem River's side.
> Again he turned himself about
>   And went the other way
> And he went south and south he went
>   And there the harbor lay!

Then Boris scratched his head and thought:
"Whatever way I go
There's always water at the end
   Whatever way I go!
New York must be an island
   An island it must be
So many people all shut in
   By rivers and by sea!

They've bridges and they've ferry boats
   Across the top to go;
They've subways and they've Hudson tubes
   To burrow down below
To get things in, to get things out
   How busy they must be!
In that enormous big New York
   On rivers and on sea!"

SPEED

This story is a definite attempt to make the child aware of a new relationship in his familiar environment.

The verse is for the older children. The story has lent itself well to dramatization.

SPEED

Once there was a big beautiful white ox. His back was broad, his horns were long and his eyes were large and gentle. He went slowly sauntering down the road one sunshiny summer day. As he walked along he swung from side to side carefully putting down his small feet. And this is what he thought:

"I am pleased with myself—so large, so broad, so strong am I. Is there anyone else who can pull so heavy a load? Is there anyone else who can plow so straight a furrow? What would the world do without me?"

Just then he heard something tearing along the road behind him. "Clopperty, clopperty, clopperty, clopperty." In a moment up dashed a big, black horse.

"Greetings," lowed the ox, slowly turning his large gentle eyes on the excited horse. "Why such haste, my brother?" The horse tossed his mane. "I'm in a hurry," he snorted, "because I'm made to go fast. Why, I can go ten miles while you crawl one! The world has no more use for a great

white snail like you. But if you want speed, I'm
just what you need. Watch how fast I go!" and
clopperty, clopperty he was off down the road.
As the ox watched the horse disappear he thought
of what he had heard.

"He called me a great white snail! He said he
could go ten miles while I crawled one! Surely
this swift horse is more wonderful than I!"

Now as the horse went frisking along this is
what he thought. "I am pleased with myself. I
am sleek, I am swift—swifter than the ox. What
would the world do without me?"

Just then he heard a strange humming overhead.
He glanced up. The sound came from a wire
taut and vibrating. Then he heard fast turning
wheels coming "Kathump, kathump." And what
do you think that poor frightened horse saw com‧
ing along the road? A self-moving car with a
trolley overhead touching the singing wire! His
eyes stuck out of his head and his mane stood on
end he was so scared. What made it go, he won‧
dered.

"Hello, clodhopper," shrieked the electric car.
"I didn't know there were any of you four-footed
curiosities left. Surely the world has no more use
for you. Where you go in half a day, I go in an
hour; where you carry one man, I carry ten. If

you want speed I'm just what you need. Just
watch me!" He was gone leaving only the humming wire overhead. The poor horse thought of
what he had heard.

"He called me a clodhopper! He said he could
go in an hour where I take half a day! Surely
this swift car is more wonderful than I!"

Now the trolley went swinging on his way thinking, "I am pleased with myself. My power is the
same as the lightning that rips the sky. I am swift,
—swifter than the ox—swifter than the horse.
What would the world do without me?"

Just then he heard a terrifying noise. It
sounded like a mightly monster coughing his life
away. "Chug, a chug a chug a chug, chug." Then
to his horror he saw coming across the green field
a gigantic iron creature with black smoke and fiery
sparks streaming from a nose on top of his head.

"Well, slowpoke," screamed the engine as he
came near the car. "Out o' breath? No wonder.
You're not made to go fast like me, for I move
by the great power of steam. Look at my monstrous boilers; see my hot fire. Where you go in
half a day, I go in an hour; where you carry one
man I carry twenty. If you want speed I'm just
what you need! Goodbye. Take your time, slow
coach." And chug, chug, he was off leaving only

a trail of dirty smoke behind him. The poor trolley car thought of what he had heard.

"He called me a slowpoke! He said he could go in an hour where I take a half day! Surely this ugly engine is greater than I!"

Now the engine raced down to the freight depot

which was near the great shipping docks. As he waited to be loaded he thought:

"I am pleased with myself. I am swift—swifter than the ox, swifter than the horse, swifter than the electric car. What would the world do without me? I serve everyone, I go everywhere——"

Just here he was interrupted by the deep boom-
ing voice of a freight steamer lying alongside the
wharf. "Tooooot" is what the voice said, "you
ridiculous landlubber! You go everywhere?
What about the water? Can you go to France and
back again? It's only I who can haul the world's
goods across the ocean! And even where you *can*
go, you never get trusted if they can possibly trust
me, now do you? Did you ever think why men use
river steamers instead of you? Did you ever think
why men cut the great Panama Canal so that sea
could flow into sea? Well, it's simply because
they're smart and prefer me to you when they can
get me. You eat too much coal with your speed,—
that's what the trouble is with you—you ridiculous
landlubber!"

This long speech made the old steamer quite
hoarse so he cleared his throat with a long
"Toooot" and sank into silence.

"Of course, what he says is true," thought the
engine. "At the same time it is equally true that
on land I *do* serve everyone, I go everywhere——"

Just here he was interrupted again by a most un-
expected noise. It sounded half like a steel giggle,
half like a brass hiccough. It made the engine un-
easy. He was sure someone was laughing at him.

Majestically he turned his headlight till it lighted up a funny little automobile who was laughing and laughing and shaking frantically like this and going "zzzzz."

"You silly little road beetle," shouted the great engine, "What on earth's the matter with you?"

The automobile gave one violent shake, turned off his spark and said in an orderly voice, "It struck my funny bone to hear you say you went everywhere *on land,* that's all. Don't you realize you're an old fuss budget with your steam and your boiler and your fire and what not? You're tied to your rails and if everything about your old tracks isn't kept just so you tumble over into a ditch or do some fool thing. Now I'm the one that can endure real hardships. Sparks and gasoline! you just sit right there, you baby, you railclinger, and watch me take that hill! Honk, honk!" And he was off up the hill.

The engine slowly turned back his headlight till the light shone full on his shiny rails. He thought of what he had heard. "He called me a rail-clinger—yes, that I am. How can that preposterous little beetle run without tracks? I'm afraid he's more wonderful than I."

Now the automobile went jouncing and bounc-

ing up the rough road puffing merrily and thinking, "I'm mightily pleased with myself. Look at
the way I climb this hill. There's nothing really
so wonderful as I——"

Just then he heard a sound that made his engine
boil with fright. Dzdzdzdzdzr—it seemed to
come right out of the sky. He got all his courage
together and turned his searchlights up. The sight
instantly killed his engine. Above him soared a
giant aeroplane. It floated, it wheeled, it rose, it
dropped. It looked serene, strong and swift.
Down, down came the great thing. Through the
terrific droning the automobile could just make
out these words:

"Dzdzdzdz. You think you're wonderful, you
poor little creeping worm tied to the earth! I pity
all you slow, slow things that I look down on as
I fly through the sky. Ox made way for horse,
horse made way for engine, car and auto but all,—
all make way for me. For if you want speed, I'm
just what you need. Dzdzdzdzdz."

And the great aeroplane wheeled and rose like a
giant bird. The automobile watched him, too
humbled to speak. Up, up, up, went the aeroplane
—up, up, up 'til it was out of sight.

SPEED

The hounds they speed with hanging tongues;
The deer they speed with bursting lungs;
    Foxes hurry,
    Field mice scurry.
    Eagles fly
    Swift, through the sky,
And man, his face all wrinkled with worry,
Goes speeding by tho' he couldn't tell why!
    But a little wild hare
    He pauses to stare
    At the daisies and baby and me
    Just sitting,—not trying to go anywhere,
    Just sitting and playing with never a care
    In the shade of a great elm tree.
    And the daisies they laugh
    As they hear the world pass,
    What is speed to the growing flowers?
    And my baby laughs
    As he sits in the grass,
    We all laugh through the sunshiny hours,—
    Through the long, dear sunshiny hours!
    For flowers and babies
    And I still know
    'Tis fun to be happy,
    'Tis fun to go slow,
    'Tis fun to take time to live and to grow.

FIVE LITTLE BABIES

This story was originally written because the children thought a negro was dirty. The songs are authentic. They have been enjoyed by children as young as four years old.

FIVE LITTLE BABIES

This is going to be a story about some little babies,—five different little babies who were born in five different parts of this big round world and didn't look alike or think alike at all.

One little baby was all yellow. He just came that way. His eyes were black and slanted up in his little face. His hair was black and straight. He wore gay little silk coats and gay little silk trousers with flowers and figures sewed all over them. When he looked up he saw his father's face was yellow and so was his mother's. And his father's hair was black and so was his mother's. And when he was a little older he saw they both wore gay silk coats and gay silk trousers with flowers and figures sewed all over them. But the baby didn't think any of this was queer,—not even when he grew up. For every one he knew had yellow skin and wore silk coats and trousers. So of course he thought all the world was that way.

But long before he was old enough to notice any of these things he knew his mother loved her little

yellow baby with slanting black eyes. And he
loved to have her take him in her arms and sing
to him, saying:

"Chu Sir Tsun Ching Min. Tsoun Sun
Gi Gi. Koo Yin Fee Min Kwei
Hua Shiang Lee Pan Run Yin.
Fon Chin Yoa Sir. Loo Yi To
Choa Yeo Liang Sung. Tsun Tze
Doo Soo Soo Wei Gun. Tsin Tsin."

For all this happened in China and he was a little
Chinese Baby.

Another little baby was all brown. He just
came that way. His eyes were black and his hair
was black. He wore pretty colored silk shawls
and little silk dresses. And when he looked up
he saw his father's face was brown and that he
wore a big turban on his head. And he saw that
around his mother's brown face was long soft
hair. He saw that she wore pretty colored silk
shawls and long silk trousers and bare feet. But
the baby didn't think any of this was queer,—even
when he grew up. He thought every one had
brown skin and that everybody dressed like himself and his father and his mother.

But long before he was old enough to notice

any of these things, he knew his mother loved her
little brown baby with black eyes. And he loved
to have her take him in her arms and sing to him,
saying:

> "Arecoco Jarecoco, Jungle parkie bare,
> Marabata cunecomunga dumrecarto sare,
> Hillee milee puneah jara de naddeah,
> Arecoco Jarecoco Jungle parkie bare."

For all this happened in India and he was a little
Indian baby.

Now another little baby was all black. He just
came that way. His eyes were black and his hair
was black and curled in tight kinky curls all over
his little head. And this little baby didn't wear
anything at all except a loin cloth. When he
looked up he saw the black faces and kinky black
hair of his father and his mother. And when
he was a little older he saw that they didn't wear
any clothes either except a loin cloth and a feather
skirt and some shells. Neither did this baby think
any of this was queer,—not even when he grew
older. He thought all the world looked and
dressed like that.

But long before he was old enough to notice
any of these things, he knew his mother loved her

little black baby with kinky black hair. And he
loved to have her take him in her arms and sing
to him, saying,

> "O túla, mntwána, O túla,
> Unyóko akamúko,
> Uséle ezintabéni,
> Uhlú shwa izigwégwe,
>   Iwá.
>
> O túla, mntwána, O túla,
> Unyóko w-zezobúya,
> Akupatéle ínto enhlé,
>   Iwá."

For all this happened in Africa and he was a little
negro baby.

Still another little baby,—he was the fourth,—
was all red. He just came that way. His eyes
were black and his hair was straight and black.
He was bound up tight and slipped into a basket
and carried around on his mother's back. He
didn't think this was queer, even when he grew
up. He thought all little babies were carried that
way. And he thought all fathers and mothers had
red skin and black hair and wore leather coats
and trousers trimmed with feathers. For his did.

But long before he was old enough to notice any
of these things he knew his mother loved her little
red baby that she carried on her back, and he

loved to have her take him out of his basket bed
and rock him in her arms and sing to him, saying:

> "Cheda-e
> Nakahu-kalu
> Be-be!
> Nakahu-kalu
> Be-be!
> E-Be-be!"

For all this happened in America long, long ago,
and he was a little Indian baby.

The last little baby, and he makes five, was all
white. He just came so too. His eyes were blue
and his hair was gold and he looked like a little
baby you know. And he wore dear little white
dresses and little knitted shoes. When he looked
up he saw his father's white skin and his mother's
blue eyes. When the baby was big enough he saw
what kind of clothes his father and his mother
wore,—but the story doesn't tell what they were
like. And when the baby was big enough he saw
they all lived in a big dirty noisy city, but the
story doesn't tell what kind of a house they lived
in. And the story doesn't tell whether he thought
any of these things queer when he was little or
when he grew up; probably because you know all
these things yourselves. But the story does tell that

long before he was old enough to notice any of
these things he knew his mother loved her little
white baby with blue eyes and golden hair.   And
it tells that he loved to have her rock him in her
arms and sing to him this song:

> "Listen, wee baby,
> I'd sing you a song;
> The arms of the mothers
> Are tender and strong,
> The arms of the mothers
> Where babies belong!
> Brown mothers and yellow
> And black and red too,
> They love their babies
> As I, dear, love you,—
> My little white blossom
> With wide eyes of blue!
> And your wee golden head,
> I do love it, I do!
> And your feet and your hands
> I love you there too!
> And my love makes me sing to you
> Sing to you songs,
> Lying hushed in my arms
> Where a baby belongs!"

For all this is happening in your own country
every day and he is a little American baby.   Perhaps you know his father,—perhaps you know the
baby,—perhaps, oh, perhaps, you have heard his
mother sing!

ONCE THE BARN WAS FULL OF HAY

This story made a special appeal to the school children because the school building was originally a
stable in MacDougal Alley. They had even wit-
nessed this evolution from stable to garage. The
children have seemed to enjoy the rhythmic language
without any sense of strangeness.

ONCE THE BARN WAS FULL OF HAY

Once the barn was full of hay,
Now 'tis there no more.
I wonder why the hay has left the barn?

The old horse stood in the stall all day.
He wanted to be on the streets.
He was strong, was this old horse.
He was wise, was this old horse.
And he was brave as well.
And he was proud, oh, very proud to be strong
        and wise and brave!
He wanted to be on the streets,
And he wondered what was wrong
That now for ten long days
No one had to come harness him up.
Old Tom, the aged driver, seemed to have gone
        away,
And only the stable boy had given him water and
        oats,
And poked him hay from the loft above.
And as the old horse thought of this

He reached up high with his quivering nose,
And pushing his lips far back on his teeth,
Pulled down a mouthful of hay.
But as he stood chewing the hay
Again he wondered and wondered again
Why nobody needed him,
Why nobody wished to drive.

For almost every day
Old Tom would harness him up
To a dear little, neat little, sweet little carriage
And down the alley they'd go and around to the
    front of the house.
And there he'd stand and wait, this dear, this
    steady old horse,
Flicking the flies with his tail,
Till the door of the house would open wide
And out would come his mistress dear with the
    baby in her arms,
And running along beside
Would come her little boy, the little boy he loved
    so well,
Who gave him sugar from his hand and patted
    his nose and neck.
And into the carriage they all would get,
His mistress and baby and little boy.
And Tom would tighten the reins a bit

And off down the street they'd go,
Clopperty, clopperty, clopperty, clop.
When he was out on the streets,—
This dear old, steady old horse,—
He knew just what to do, when to go and when
to stand still.
And when with clang! clang! clang!
Fire engines shrieked down the street
He'd stand as still as a rock
So his mistress and her baby were never frightened
a bit!
And the little boy laughed and watched and
laughed!
And when the great policeman, so big in the
middle of the street,
Held up his hand,
The old horse stopped
But watched him close
For the first wave of the hand that would tell him
to go ahead.
Always the first to stop,
Always the first to go,
The old horse loved the streets.

Now he wanted the streets.
And while he stood and chewed his hay and wondered what was wrong,

Suddenly there came a rumble
Of noises all a-jumble,
A quaking and a shaking
A terrifying tremble
Making the old horse quiver and stand still!
It came from the alley,
His own peaceful alley
Where he knew every horse, every coach, every
      wagon!
Bump, thump, like a lump of lead jolting,
Bang, whang, like a steam engine bolting,
Down it came crashing
Down it came smashing,
Till it stopped with a snort at his own stable door!
The old horse pulled at his halter
And strained to look round at the door.
Out of the tail of his eye he could see
The doors, the doors to his very own barn,
Swing wide under the crane where they hoisted
      the hay.
And there in the alley, oh what did he see
This old horse with his terrified eye?
A monster all shiny and black
With great headlights stuck way out in front,
With brass things that grated and groaned
As the driver pulled this thing and that.
And there on the back of this monster

Sat old Tom
Who had driven him now for fifteen long years.
And out of the mouth of the monster, as there
    opened a neat little door,
Stepped his mistress dear
With her eager little boy and the baby in her arms.
And the poor horse trembled to see those that he
    loved so well
So near this terrible monster.
" 'Twill eat them all!" he thought.
And for the first time in all his brave and prudent
    life
The old horse was frightened.
He raised his head,
He spread his nostrils,
He neighed with all his strength.
His mistress dear
Would surely hear,
Would hear and understand!
He wanted to save her, save the boy and save the
    little baby
From this terrible ugly beast
Snorting there so near!
And his mistress dear, she heard.
But did she understand?
She came and laid her hand upon his quivering
    side.

"Poor dear old horse," she said,
"Your day is gone and you must go!"
What could she mean?
What could she mean?
What could she mean?
"You have been strong; but not so strong as is our
    new machine!
You have been brave; but see this thing, this thing
    can know no fear!
You have been wise; but this machine is like a
    part of Tom.
He pulls a lever, turns a wheel and this machine
    obeys!
Poor dear old horse
Your day is gone
And now you too must go!"
So that was what she meant!
So that was what she meant!
So that was what she meant!

The old horse heard but how could he under-
    stand?
How could he know that she had said
They wanted him no longer?
How could he know that this big monster, this
    new automobile
Was going to do his work for them

And do it better than he!
He knew that something was wrong.
He was puzzled and sad and frightened.
With head drooped low and feet that dragged
He let old Tom untie his rope
And lead him from the stall.
For one short moment as he passed the shiny
  automobile
He straightened his head and widened his nostrils
And snorted and snorted again.
But there within the monster, lying safe upon a
  seat,
He saw the little baby
Laughing and all alone.
And the old horse was puzzled, was puzzled and
  frightened too.
Then old Tom pulled him gently through the wide
  swinging doors
And led him down the alley.
Past the stables with other horses,
Past the grooms and stable boys,
Down the alley he knew so well
Went the old horse for the last time.
For he never came back again.
They had no need of him; they liked their auto
  better!
Down the alley he slowly went

And as he turned into the street below
One last long look he gave to the stable at the end,
One last long look at his mistress dear with the
      baby in her arms,
One last long look at the little boy waving and
      calling: "Goodbye, goodbye"
One last long look, and then he was gone!

Once the barn was full of hay:
Now 'tis there no more.
I wonder why the hay has left the barn?

THE WIND

This story is composed entirely of observations on the wind dictated by a six-year-old and a seven-year-old class. Every phrase (except the one word "toss") is theirs. The ordering only is mine.

.

THE WIND

In the summer-time the wind goes like breathing,
But in a winter storm it growls and roars.

Sometimes the wind goes oo-oo-oo-oo-oo! It
sounds like water running. It makes a singing
sound. It blows through the grass. It blows

against the tree and the tree bows over and bends
way down. It whistles in the leaves and makes
a rustling sound. The tree shakes, the branches

and leaves all rustle. The wind knocks the leaves
off the trees and tosses them up in the air. Then
it blows them straight in to the window and drags
them around on the floor. It makes the leaves
whirl and twirl.

And sometimes the wind is frisky. It whisks
around the corners. It comes blowing down the
street. It blows the papers round and round on
the ground. It tears them and rares them, then
up, it takes them sailing. It sweeps around the
house, blowing and puffing. It blows the wash
up. It blows the chickens off the trees. It makes
the nuts come rattling down. It turns the wind-
mill and makes the fire burn. It blows out the
matches, it blows out the candles, it blows out the
gas lights. It hits the people on the street. Some
it keeps back from walking and some it pushes
forward. It unbuttons the coat of a little girl, it
unbuttons her leggings too and the little girl feels
all chilly in the frisky wind. It blows up her
skirt. It pulls off her hat and blows through her
hair till she feels all chilly on her head too. Puff!
it goes, puff! puff! Then off go other hats spinning down the street. It gets under umbrellas and
turns them inside out. The frisky wind blows
harder and harder. The houses shake. The win-

dows rattle. And the people on the street are whirling and twirling like the leaves.

Sometimes there is a storm. The wind roars over the ocean and makes the waves bigger than the ships. The waves go up and down, and up and down, and the ship goes rocking and rocking, this way and that way, this way and that way, to the right, to the left, to the right, to the left, back and forth and back and forth. A boat gets tossed on the sea. The sails are all torn to pieces by the storm. The masts get broken off and fall down on the ship. The ship just rocks and rocks. Then pretty soon it bumps into a rock and is wrecked and sinks. And all the men get drowned.

The wind growls and roars over the mountain. There is thunder and lightning. The thunder says, "Boompety, boom, boom, boom!" The lightning is all shiny. The rain comes pouring down. The wind whistles in the trees. It blows a tree over. It crashes down. The lightning goes crack! and splits the tree in two. And then the tree catches on fire and the leaves burn like paper.

In the summer-time the wind goes like breathing,
But in a winter storm it growls and roars.

THE LEAF STORY

All the content and many of the expressions were taken from stories on dried leaves dictated by a six-year-old and a seven-year-old class.

THE LEAF STORY

I want to fly up in the air!
If I take two leaves in my hands and put two leaves
      on my feet
And the wind blows
Perhaps I'll fly up in the air!

Listen!
Something stirs in the dried leaves,
The tree bends, the tree bows,

The wind sweeps through the brown leaves.
The brown leaves crackle and rattle and dance,
They rustle and murmur and pull at the bough,
They shiver, they quiver till they pull themselves
      loose
And are free.
Up, up they fly!
Little brown specks in the sky.
They twist and they spin,
They whirl and they twirl,
They teeter, they turn somersaults in the air.
Then for a moment the wind holds its breath.
Down, down, down float the leaves,
Still turning and twisting,
Still twirling and whirling,
The brown leaves float to the earth.
Puff! goes the wind,
Up they fly again
With a little soft rustling laugh.
Then down they float.
Down, down, down.
On the ground the leaves go as if walking or
      running.
They go and then they stop.
They scurry along,
Still twisting and turning,
Still twirling and whirling,

They hurry along,
With a soft little rustle
They tumble, they roll and they roll.

I want to fly up in the air!
If I take two leaves in my hands and put two
      leaves on my feet
And the wind blows,
Perhaps I'll fly up in the air.

A LOCOMOTIVE

In the daytime, what am I?
In the hubbub, what am I?
A mass of iron and of steel,
Of boiler, piston, throttle, wheel,
A monster smoking up the sky,
   A locomotive!
    That am I!

In the darkness, what am I?
In the stillness, what am I?
Streak of light across the sky,
A clanging bell, a shriek, a cry,
A fiery demon rushing by,
   A locomotive
    That am I!

MOON MOON

(To the tune of "Du, du, liegst mir im herzen.")

Moon, moon,
  Shiny and silver,
Moon, moon,
  Silver and white;
Moon, moon,
  Whisper to children
  "Sleep through the silvery night."
There, there, there, there,
  Sleep through the silvery night.

Sun, sun,
  Shiny and golden,
Sun, sun,
  Golden and gay;
Sun, sun,
  Shout to the children
  "Wake to the sunshiny day!"
There, there, there, there,
  Wake to the sunshiny day.

AUTOMOBILE SONG

A-rolling, bowling, fast or slow,
A-racing, chasing, off we go.
The jolly automobile
Whizzes along with flying wheel.
We go chug, chug-chug, chug-up!
Then we go s-l-i-d-i-n-g down.
We go scooting over the hills,
We go tooting back to town.

SILLY WILL

In this story I have used a device to tie together many isolated familiar facts. I have never found that six-year-old children did not readily discriminate the actual from the imaginary.

SILLY WILL

Part I

Once there was a little boy. Now he was a very silly little boy, so silly that he was called Silly Will. He had an idea that he was tremendously smart and that he could quite well get along by himself in this world. This foolish idea made him do and say all sorts of silly things which led to all sorts of terrible happenings as this story will show.

One day he went out walking. He walked down the road until he met a little girl. The little girl was crying.

"What's the matter with you?" asked Silly Will.

"Oh!" sobbed the little girl, "our cow has died and I don't know what we shall do. I don't know how we can get along without her milk and everything. We depended on her so!"

"Depended on a cow!" cried Silly Will. "Whoever heard of such a thing! I've often seen that stupid old cow of yours. Clumsy, lumbering thing! Cows are no good! I wouldn't depend on

any animal, not I! It wouldn't matter to me if all
the cows in the world died!" And Silly Will
strutted off down the road.

The little girl looked after him with astonish-
ment. "I just wish no cow would ever give that
silly boy anything!" she thought.

Before long he met an old woman. The old
woman was crying too.

"What's the matter with you?" asked Silly Will.

"Oh!" cried the old woman wringing her hands.
"Our sheep has fallen over a cliff and broken its
legs and it's going to die. I don't know how we
shall get along without her wool for spinning. We
depended so much on her!"

"Depended on a sheep!" cried Silly Will.
"Whoever heard of such a thing! I've often heard
your stupid old sheep bleating. Sheep are no
good. I wouldn't depend on any animal, not I!
It wouldn't matter to me if all the sheep in the
world died!" And Silly Will strutted off down
the road feeling very smart.

The old woman looked after him greatly surprised. "Silly little boy!" she thought. "He little knows! I just wish no sheep would give him
anything!"

Then before long Silly Will met a man. The

man was sitting beside the road with his face in his hands.

"What's the matter with you?" asked Silly Will.

The man looked up. "Oh, our horse has died!" he sighed dolefully, "and I don't know how we can get along without him to plow for us now that it's seeding time. And there's not much use getting in the seeds anyway without a horse to carry the grain to market when it's ripe. We depended so on our horse!"

"Depended on a horse!" cried Silly Will. "Whoever heard of such a thing! First I meet a little girl who says she depended on a cow for food: then I meet an old woman who says she depended on a sheep for clothes. And here is a man who says he depends on a horse to work and to carry for him! As for me, I depend on no animal, not I! It wouldn't matter to me if there were no animals in the world. They needn't give me anything! I wish they wouldn't!"

The man looked at him greatly amazed. "Silly little boy!" he said. "I hope your silly wish will come true. How little you understand! I just wish tonight all the animal kingdom would leave you and then perhaps you would understand a little!" But Silly Will walked home feeling very smart, for he *didn't* understand. Silly people never *do* understand!

Now that night a strange thing happened to Silly Will. I can't explain how or why it happened. But in the middle of the night, all the animals *did* leave Silly Will. Not only the cow and the sheep and the horse but all the animal kingdom! He was sound asleep in his flannel nightgown snuggled under warm wool blankets. Suddenly he felt a jerk. What was happening? He sat up in bed just in time to see his blankets whisk off him and disappear. He looked down. His night shirt was gone! He heard a faint sound almost like the bleating of the old woman's sheep. "Ba-ba-a-a I take back my wool!"

Then he was aware that something queer had happened to his mattress. It was just an empty bag of ticking. He heard a faint sound almost like the neighing of the man's horse who had died. "Whey-ey-ey, I take back my hair!"

He reached for his pillow. It too was an empty sack.

"Hh-ss-s-hh" hissed a faint sound almost like a goose. "I take back my feathers!"

"Whatever is happening?" screamed Silly Will. "Let me get a light." He found a match and struck it, but his candlestick was empty. "Ba-*r*-

moo-oo" said some faint voices. "I take back my
fat!"

By this time Silly Will was thoroughly frightened and shivering with cold besides.

"I'd better get dressed," he thought, and groped
his way to the chair where he had left his clothes.
He could find only his cotton underwaist and his
cotton shirt. His wool undershirt and drawers,
his trousers and stockings, and his silk necktie were
gone. And so were his leather shoes. Just the
lacings lay on the floor. "Mooooo" he seemed to
hear a faint sound almost like the little girl's cow
he had made fun of in the afternoon. "I take back
my hide."

He put on the few cotton clothes that were left,
but there were no buttons to hold them together.
"Moooooo," he heard a faint voice say. "I take
back my bones."

Terrified he ran to the closet to see what more he
could find. "I'll surely freeze," he thought as he
lighted another match. "I'll slip on my coat and
get into bed." But his warm coat with the fur col-
lar was gone, too. "Chee, chee, chee," he seemed
to hear a faint sound almost like the squirrel he was
fond of frightening. "I take back my skin!"

But he did find some cotton stockings and some
old overalls. These he put on relieved to find they

had metal buttons. Then poor Silly Will crawled back to bed wearing his cotton clothes and waited for morning to come. He didn't sleep much for the wire spring cut into him. He was cold, too.

As soon as it was light he hunted around for more clothes. He found some straw bed-room slippers. His rubbers too were there and he put them on over his slippers. Then he ran downstairs to get something to eat.

"Anyway," he thought, "those old animals can't get me when it comes to eating. I never did care much about meat."

The pantry door squeaked as he opened it. It sounded for all the world like a far away barnyard —hens, cows, and pigs. He looked around. No milk, no eggs, no bacon! "Bread and butter will do me," he thought.

But the butter had gone too! He opened the bread box. The bread was still there! He almost wept from relief. By hunting around he found a good deal to eat. Cocoa made with water instead of milk was pretty good. Then there were crackers and apples. His oatmeal wasn't very good without milk or butter. But he ate it. He knew he would have plenty of vegetables and fruits and cereals.

And the day was warm enough so that he didn't

mind his cotton clothes. But his feet did hurt him. He wondered about wooden shoes and thought he would try to make some.

He was a little worried too about his bed. He hunted around in the house until he found two cotton comforters. One he put under his sheet in place of his mattress and one on top in place of his blankets. So, on the whole, he thought, he could manage to get along.

Poor little Silly Will! He had never before thought how much the animals did for him. Once in a while he would think of the little girl and the old woman and the man he had met that afternoon. But not for long. And he never remembered that some time winter would come. But long before that time came, Silly Will had got himself into still more trouble. For even now he didn't understand!

PART 2

From this time on nothing went well with Silly Will. When he had eaten the vegetables he had in the house he walked over to a gardener who lived nearby. He wanted to get potatoes and other sup-

plies for the winter. To his horror he found everything drooping and wilted and withered. "What's
the matter with the vegetables, gardener?" asked
Silly Will.

"A frost," sighed the gardener. "It's killed all
the potatoes. I hope you weren't depending on
them?"

"Oh, of course not," said Silly Will, gulping
hard. "I certainly wouldn't depend on a vegetable.
That would be too ridiculous. If the frost should
kill all the vegetables, it would make no difference
to me!" Nevertheless in his heart he felt unhappy
and a little frightened at the thought of the coming winter. But still he didn't understand. Silly
people never do understand.

He walked on down the road saying to himself,
"I'll go order my winter wood anyway. I'm almost
out of it at home." Just then he looked up. He
expected to see the green forest stretching up the
hillside. He stared. The hillside was black smoking stumps, fallen blackened trees, white ashes!
Beside the dead trees stood the old forester wringing his hands. Silly Will didn't even speak to him.
He could see what had happened without asking.
He turned around. Slowly he walked home. He
went right to bed. He still pretended that he
wasn't unhappy or frightened. He kept saying to

himself, "I don't really depend on the wood at all. Of course that would be silly! I've got coal. It wouldn't matter to me if all the plants left me." And with that thought he fell asleep. You see even now he didn't understand. Silly people never do understand.

Now that night another strange thing happened to Silly Will. I can't explain how or why it happened. But in the middle of the night all the plants *did* leave Silly Will,—not only the potatoes and the trees but the whole vegetable kingdom.

He was asleep all curled up to keep warm in his cotton clothes. Suddenly he felt the comforter and sheet under him jerk away and he was left lying on the wire spring. At the same time the comforter and sheet over him disappeared. So did his nightshirt. Then bang! His wooden bed was gone. The house began to creak and rock. He jumped up and tore down stairs. He just got outside the front door when the whole house collapsed.

The moon was shining. Silly Will could see quite plainly. There stood the brick chimneys rising out of a pile of plaster dumped on top of the concrete foundations. There was the slate roof and the broken window of glass. The air was full of a sound like the violent trembling of many leaves. It sounded for all the world as if it said, "I take back my wood!"

"Whatever will I do?" groaned Silly Will as he shivered all naked in the moonlight. Then his eye lighted on the kitchen stove. There it stood with the stove pipe all safely connected with the chimney.

"I'll build a coal fire," he thought. There stood the iron coal scuttle. But alas! It was empty! He heard a far-away murmur like a faint wind stirring in giant ferns. And they said, "I take back my buried leaves!"

By this time Silly Will was shaking with cold. "I've heard that newspapers are warm," he thought. But the pile behind the stove was gone. Again came the murmur of trees—"I take back my pulp," and a queer soft sound which he couldn't quite make out. Was it "I take back my cotton?"

Silly Will was thoroughly terrified now.

"I'll go somewhere to think," he said to himself. So he crept down the cement steps to the cellar and crawled into a sheltered corner. But he couldn't think of anything pleasant. He could hear a confused noise all around him. Sometimes it sounded like growls, like animal cries, like animal calls. "The animal kingdom has left him," it seemed to say.

Again it sounded like the wind rustling a thousand leaves. "The vegetable kingdom has left him," it seemed to say.

"I've nothing to wear," sobbed Silly Will. "And I'm afraid I've nothing to eat." At the thought of food he jumped up and ran over to the cellar pantry. He found just three things. They did not make a tempting meal! They were a crock of salt, a tin of soda and a porcelain pitcher of water.

"What shall I ever do? How shall I live? I'll never have another glass of milk or cup of cocoa. I'll never have anything to wear. I'll freeze and I'll starve. I might just as well die now!" And poor little Silly Will broke down and cried and cried and cried.

"I can't live without other living things," he sobbed. "I can't eat only minerals and I can't keep warm in minerals. Everybody has to depend on animals and vegetables. And after all I'm only a little boy! I've got to have living things to keep alive myself!"

Then a wonderful thing happened to Silly Will. I can't explain how or why it happened. Suddenly he felt all warm and comfortable. "Perhaps I'm freezing," he thought. "I've heard that people feel warm when they are almost frozen to death."

Slowly he put out his hand. Surely that was a

linen sheet! Surely that was a woolen blanket.
Surely he had on his flannel nightgown. He sat
straight up. Surely this was his own bed: this was
his own room: this was his own house. He could
scarcely believe his eyes. He gave a great shout.

"Moo-oo-oo," answered a cow under a tree outside his window. And the leaves of the tree rustled
at him too.

"Hello, old cow! Hello, old tree!" cried Silly
Will running to the window. "Isn't it good we're
all alive?" And when you think of it that wasn't
a silly remark at all!

"Moo-oo-oo," lowed the old cow. "Swish-sh-
sh-sh," rustled the tree. And suddenly Silly Will
thought he understood! I wonder if he did!

EBEN'S COWS

This story attempts to make an industrial process a background for real adventure.

EBEN'S COWS

PART 1

Eben was looking at the cows. And the cows were looking at Eben. What Eben saw was twenty-six pairs of large gentle eyes, twenty-six mouths chewing with a queer sidewise motion, twenty-six fine fat cattle, some red, some white, some black, some red and white, and some black and white, all in a bright green meadow. What the cows saw, held by his mother on the rail fence, was a fat baby with a shining face and waving arms. What Eben heard was the heavy squashy footsteps of the slow-moving cows as they lumbered toward the little figure on the fence. What the cows heard was a high, excited little voice saying a real word for the first time in its life, "Cow! cow! oh, cow! oh, cow!" And so with his first word began Eben's life-long friendship with the cows.

Eben Brewster lived in a little white farm-house with green blinds. The cows lived in a great long red barn, which was connected with the little white farm-house by a wagon-shed and tool-house. High up on the great red barn was printed GREEN

MOUNTAIN FARM. Long before Eben knew
how to read he knew what those big letters said,
and he knew that the lovely rolling hills that
ringed the farm around, were called the Green
Mountains. In front of both house and barn
stretched the bright green meadows where day
after day fed the twenty-six cows. In a neighbor-

ing meadow played the long-legged calves. For
at Green Mountain Farm there were always many
calves. In the summer they usually had fifteen
or twenty calves a few months old. For every cow
of course had her baby once a year. The little

bull calves they sold; but the little cow calves they raised.

When Eben was three years old he made friends with the calves his own way. He wiggled through the bars of the gate into their pasture. The calves stared at him; they sniffed at him. Then they came a little closer. They stared at him again. They sniffed at him again. Then they came closer still. Then one little black and white thing came right up to him and licked his face and hands. And three-year-old Eben liked the feel of the soft nose and the rough tongue and he liked the sweet cow smell.

So it came about that Eben played regularly with the calves. It always amused his father Andrew to watch them together. "I never saw a child so crazy about cows!" he used to say. One day he put a pretty little new calf,—white with red spots,—into the pasture. Eben ran to the calf at once. "What shall we call the calf, Eben?" asked his father. "Think of some nice name for her." Eben put his arms around the calf's neck and smiled. "I call him 'ittle Sister," he said. For little baby sister was the only thing three-year-old Eben loved better than a calf. And the name stuck to the calves of Green Mountain Farm. From that time on they were always called Little Sisters!

Real little sister or Nancy, as she was called, grew apace. To her Eben was always wonderful. At six years he seemed equal to about anything. It did not surprise her at all one day to hear her father say, "Eben, you get the cows to-night." But it did surprise Eben. He had helped his father drive them home for years. And now he was to do it alone! Down the dusty road he went, switch in hand, taking such big important strides that the footprints of his little bare feet were almost as far apart as a man's. The cows stood facing the bars. He took down the bars. The cows filed through one by one. Nancy and her father, waiting to help him turn the cows in at the barn, knew he was coming. They could see the cloud of dust and hear the many shuffling feet and the shrill boy's voice calling: "Hi, Spotty, don't you stop to eat! Go 'long there, Crumplehorn, don't you know the way home yet! Hurry up, Redface. Can't you keep in the road?" Eben felt older from that day.

From the day he began driving home the cows alone Eben took a real share in the work at the farm. He put the cows' heads into the stanchions when each one lumbered into her stall. He fed them hay and ensilage through the long winter months when the meadows were white with snow.

He put the cans to catch the cream and the
skimmed milk when his father turned the separator. He took the separator apart and carried
it up to his mother to be washed. Nancy helped
and talked. Only she really talked more than she
helped!

Eben's talk ran much on cows. His poor
mother read all she could in the encyclopedia, but
even then she couldn't answer all his questions.
Why does a cow have four stomachs? Why does
her food come back to be chewed? Why does
she chew sideways? Why does she have to be
milked twice a day? Why doesn't she get out of
the way when an auto comes down the road?
When Eben asked his father these things the
farmer would shake his head and answer, "I guess
it's just because she's a cow."

There came a very exciting day at Green
Mountain Farm. For twenty years Andrew
Brewster and his men had milked his cows morning and evening. His hands were hard from the
practice. The children loved to watch him milk.
With every pull of his strong hands he made a
fine white stream of milk shoot into the pail, squirt,
squirt, squirt. Eben had often tried, but pull as
he would, he could only get out a few drops. And
even as Andrew Brewster had milked his cows

morning and evening until his hands were horny, so had his father done before him. Yes, and his father's father, too. For three generations of Brewsters had hardened their hands milking cows on Green Mountain Farm. Then there came this exciting day, and a new way of milking began at the big red barn.

A milking machine was put in. It ran by a wonderful little puffing gasolene engine. It milked two cows at once. And it milked all twenty-six of them in twenty minutes. Andrew Brewster could manage the whole herd alone with what help Eben could give him. It was a great day for him. It was a great day for Eben and Nancy too.

PART 2

There came another day which was even more exciting for the two children than when the milking machine was put into the big red barn. This story is really about that day. Eben was then ten years old and Nancy seven. Their father and mother had gone for the day to a county fair. The two children were to be alone all day, which made up for not going to the fair. The children had long since eaten the cold dinner their mother had left for them. They had done all their chores too. Nancy had gathered the eggs and Eben had chopped the kindling and brought in the wood. They had fed the baby chickens and given them water. Then they had gone to the woods for an afternoon climb over the big rocks and a wade in the brook. Now they were waiting for their father and mother to come back. They had been waiting for a long time, for it was seven o'clock. The last thing their mother had called out as she drove off behind the two old farm horses was, "We'll be back by five o'clock, children."

What could have happened? "Eben," said Nancy, "we'd better eat our own supper and get something ready for Father and Mother. I guess I'll try to scramble some eggs."

"Go ahead," answered Eben. "But we're not the ones I'm worrying about—nor Father and Mother either. It's those poor cows."

"Oh! the cows!" cried Nancy. "And the poor Little Sisters! They'll be so hungry." Both children ran to the door. "Just listen to them," said Eben. "They've been waiting in the barn for over an hour now. I certainly wish Father would come." From the big red barn came the lowing of the restless cattle. "I'm going to have another look at them," said Eben. "Come along, Nancy."

The two children peered into the big dark barn.
The unmistakable cow smell came to them strong
in the dark. Stretching down the whole length
was stall after stall, each holding an impatient
cow. The children could see the restless hind feet
moving and stamping; they could see the flicking
of many tails; they could feel the cows pulling
at the stanchions. On the other side were the stalls
of the Little Sisters. They too were moving about
wildly. Over above it all rose the deafening sound
of the plaintive lowings. By the door stood the
gasolene engine. It was attached to a pipe which
ran the whole length of the great barn above the
cows' stalls. Eben's eyes followed this pipe until
it was lost in the dark.

"Moo-oo-oo," lowed the cow nearest at hand, so
loud that both children jumped. "Poor old Redface," said Nancy. "I wish we could help you."
"We're going to," said Eben in an excited voice.
"See here, Nancy. We're going to milk these
cows!" "Why, Eben Brewster, we could never
do it alone!" Nancy's eyes went to the gasolene
engine as she spoke. "We've got to," said Eben.
"That's all there is about it."

So the children began with trembling hands.
They lighted two lanterns. "I wish the cows
would stop a minute," said Nancy. "I can't seem

to think with such a racket going on." Eben
turned on the spark of the engine. He had done
it before, but it seemed different to do it when his
father wasn't standing near. Then he took the
crank. "I hope she doesn't kick tonight," he
wished fervently. He planted his feet firmly and
grasped the handle! Round he swung it, around
and around. Only the bellowing of the cows answered. He began again. Round he swung the
handle; around and around. "Chug, chug-a-chug,
chug, chug, chug-a-chug, chug," answered the engine. Nancy jumped with delight. "You're as
good as a man, Eben," she cried.

"Come now, bring the lantern," commanded
Eben. Nancy carried the lantern and Eben a rubber tube. This tube Eben fastened on to the first
faucet on the long pipe between the first two cows.
This rubber tube branched into two and at the end
of each were four hollow rubber fingers. Eben
stuck his fingers down one. He could feel the air
pull, pull, pull. "She's working all right, Nancy,"
he whispered in a shaking voice. "Put the pail
here." Nancy obeyed. Eben took one bunch of
four hollow rubber fingers and slipped one finger
up each udder of one cow. Then he took the other
bunch and slipped one finger up each udder of
the second cow. The cows, feeling relief was near,

quieted at once. "I can see the milk," screamed
Nancy, watching a tiny glass window in the rubber tube. And sure enough, through the tube and
out into the pail came a pulsing stream of milk.
Squirt, squirt, squirt, squirt. In a few minutes
the two cows were milked and the children moved
on to the next pair. Nancy carried the pail and
Eben the rubber tube which he fastened on to the
next faucet. And in another few minutes two
more cows were milked. So the children went the
length of the great red barn, and gradually the
restless lowings quieted as pail after pail was filled
with warm white milk.

"I wouldn't try the separator if it weren't for
the poor Little Sisters," said Eben anxiously as
they reached the end of the barn. "They've got
to be fed," said Nancy. "But I can't lift those
pails." Slowly Eben carried them one by one with
many rests back to the separator by the gasoline
engine. He took the strap off one wheel and put
it around the wheel of the separator. "I can't
lift a whole pail," sighed Eben. Taking a little
at a time he poured the milk into the tray at the
top of the separator. In a few minutes the yellow cream came pouring out of one spout and the
blue skimmed milk out of another. In another
few minutes the calves were drinking the warm

skimmed milk. "There, Little Sisters, poor, hungry Little Sisters," said Nancy, as she watched their eager pink tongues.

Eben turned off the engine. "I'm sorry I couldn't do the final hand milking," he said. "I wonder if we'd better turn the cows out?" Before Nancy could answer both children heard a sound. They held their breath. Surely those were horses' feet! Cloppety clop clop clop cloppety clop clop clop. Up to the barn door dashed the old farm horses. From the dark outside the children heard their mother's voice, "Children, children, are you there? The harness broke and I thought we'd *never* get home." Carrying a lantern apiece the children rushed out and into her arms. "Here, Eben," called his father. "You take the horses quick. I must get started milking right away. Those poor cows!" The children were too excited to talk plainly. They both jabbered at once. Then each took a hand of their father and led him into the great red barn. There by the light of the lanterns Andrew Brewster could see the pails of warm white milk and yellow cream. He stared at the quiet cows and at the Little Sisters. Then he stared at Eben and Nancy. "Yes," cried both children together. "We did it. We did it ourselves!"

THE SKY SCRAPER

The story tries to assemble into a related form many facts well-known to seven-year-olds and to present the whole as a modern industrial process.

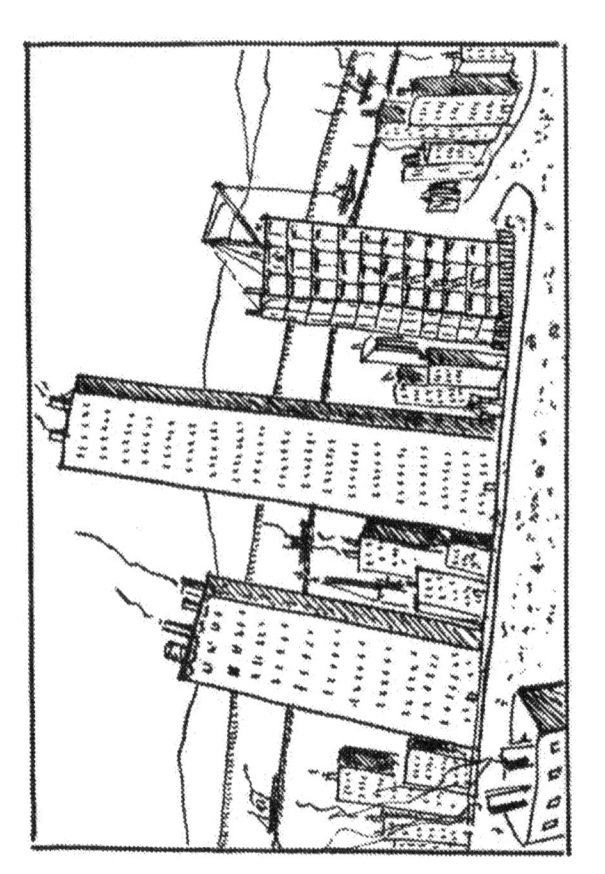

THE SKY SCRAPER

Once in an enormous city, men built an enormous building. Deep they built it, deep into the ground; high they built it, high into the air. Now that it is finished the men who walk about its feet forget how deep into the ground it reaches. But they can never forget how high into the blue it soars. Their necks ache when they throw back their heads to see to the top. For, of all the buildings in the world, this sky scraper is the highest.

The sky scraper stands in the heart of the great city. From its top one can see the city, one can hear the city, one can smell the city—the city where men live and work. One can see the crowded streets full of tiny men and tiny automobiles, the riverside with its baby warehouses and its baby docks, the river with its toy bridges and toy giant steamers and tug boats and barges and ferries. The city noise,—the distant, rumbling, grumbling noise,—sounds like the purring of a far-away giant beast. And over it all lies the smell of gas and smoke.

The sky scraper stands in the heart of the great

city. But from its top in the blue, blue sky one can see all over the land. Landward the fields spread out like a map till they are lost in the mist and smoke. Seaward lies the vast, the tremendous stretch of the sea, the wrinkled, the crinkled, the far-away sea that stretches to touch the sky.

Now this soaring sky scraper is the work of men —of many, many men. Its lofty lacy tower was first thought of by the architect. With closed eyes he saw it, and with his well-trained fingers quickly he drew its outline. Then at his office many men with T squares and with compasses, sitting at high long tables, with green-shaded lamps, worked far into the nights till all the plans were ready.

Then the sky scraper began to grow. The first men brought mighty steam shovels. One hundred feet into the earth they burrowed. The gigantic mouths of the steam shovels gnawed at the rock and the clay. Huge hulks they clutched from this underworld, heaved up with enormous derricks and crashed out on the upper land. Deep they dug, deep into the ground till they found the firm bed-rock. With a network of steel they filled this terrific hole. Into the rasping, revolving mixers they poured tons of sand and cement and gravel which steadily flowed in a sluggish stream to strengthen the steel supports.

At last,—and that was an exciting day,—the great beams began to rise. Again the derricks ground, as slowly, steadily, accurately, they swung each beam to its place. A thousand men swarmed over the steel bones, some throwing red-hot rivets, others catching them in pails, all to the song of the rivet driver.

The riveter screamed and shrieked and shrilled. It pierced the air of the narrow streets. On the

nearby buildings it vibrated, echoed. The sky scraper seemed alive and thrilled by the quiver-

ing, throbbing, shrieking shrill,—by the song of
the riveter. Story by story the sky scraper grew,
a monstrous outline against the sky. And ever and
ever as it grew, hissed the rivet and screamed the
drill.

At length the sky scraper soared sixty dizzy
stories high. Then swiftly came the stone masons
and encased the giant steel frame. Swiftly in its
center, men reared the plunging elevators. Swiftly
worked the electrician, the plumber, the carpenter. All workmen were called and all workmen
came. The world listened to the call of this sky
scraper standing in the heart of the great city.
From the mines of Minnesota to the swamps of
Louisiana came goods to serve its need. Long,
long ago, in olden days, the churches grew slowly
bit by bit, as one man carved a door post here and
another fitted a window there, each planning his
own part. Not so with the sky scraper. It grew
in haste. Its parts were made in factories scattered
the country over. Each factory was ready with a
part, and the railroad was ready swift to bring
them to its feet. The sky scraper grew in haste.
For it the many worked as one.

Planned by those who command and reared by
those who obey, in an enormous city men built this
enormous building. Deep they built it, deep into

the ground; high they built it, high into the air.
And now they use this building built by them.

The sky scraper houses an army of ten thousand
men. All day they clamber up and down its core

like insects in a giant tree. They buzz and buzz, and then go home.

But there with the shadowy silent streets at its feet stands the lofty sky scraper. On its head there glows a monstrous light. The rays pierce through the fogs. And when the storm is screaming wild, the light struggles through to the frightened boats tossing on the mountain waves. The storm howls and beats on the sides of the lofty lacy tower with the shining light on top. The storms beat on its side, the tower leans in the wind, the tower of steel and of stone leans and leans a full two feet. Then when the blast is past, this tower of steel and of stone swings back to straightness again.

And so in the enormous city men built this enormous building. Deep they built it, deep into the ground; high, they built it, high into the air. Now that it is finished, the men who walk about its feet forget how deep into the ground it reaches. But they can never forget how high into the blue it soars. Their necks ache when they throw back their heads to see to the top. For of all the build‐ings in the world this sky scraper is the highest.

END

Lightning Source UK Ltd.
Milton Keynes UK
UKHW010812151022
410493UK00001B/363